The PERFECT LOVE SONG

The PERFECT
LOVE SONG

A Holiday Story

PATTI CALLAHAN HENRY

Published by Vanguard Press
A Member of the Perseus Books Group

Designed by Trish Wilkinson
Set in 12 point Centaur MT

Library of Congress Cataloging-in-Publication Data

Henry, Patti Callahan.
    The perfect love song : a holiday story / Patti Callahan Henry.
        p.   cm.
    ISBN 978-1-59315-616-9 (alk. paper)
    1. Christmas stories. I. Title.
PS3608.E578P47 2010
813'.6—dc22   2010019377

Vanguard Press books are available at special discounts for bulk purchases in the U.S. by corporations, institutions, and other organizations. For more information, please contact the Special Markets Department at the Perseus Books Group, 2300 Chestnut Street, Suite 200, Philadelphia, PA 19103, or call (800) 810-4145, ext. 5000, or e-mail special.markets@perseusbooks.com.

10 9 8 7 6 5 4 3 2 1

To my reader:
this story is my love song to you.
And
to Kimberly Whalen,
my extraordinary agent, who, since my first novel,
has traveled with me on this writing journey
and encouraged me to write this very
particular story at this very particular time.

May stillness be upon your thoughts and silence upon your tongue!
For I tell you a tale that was told at the beginning . . .
the one story worth the telling.

—A TRADITIONAL IRISH STORYTELLER'S OPENING

CHAPTER ONE

*The truth inside the story is
what the storyteller aims for . . .*
—Maeve Mahoney to Kara Larson

Jimmy Sullivan—God bless his soul—wrote the perfect Christmas song. Now, I'm not the only one who says this, so don't go thinking this is just my opinion. This was so perfect a song that it almost ruined him.

When Jimmy wrote this song it was his first holiday season with Charlotte. Well, not technically his first, but when it comes to storytelling I'm not really sure if the word "technically" should enter our minds or hearts. Pure love formed this song. Of course, this is where the best stories,

I

melodies, and lyrics are born: love. You might not believe that a mere song can change a life, but I'm here to tell you that it can and it did.

$\mathscr{I}$t was Thanksgiving morning when the Unknown Souls band tour bus pulled up to the Larson family house. Brothers Jack and Jimmy Sullivan were asleep in the backseat, exhausted after their Savannah concert the previous night. It was a balmy coastal morning in Palmetto Pointe, South Carolina, the air infused with the rain of the past two weeks. The palms bent low in submission from the constant beating of wind and rain, the ground damp with the sweet smell of earth, sea, and life combined—an aroma of their childhood.

Jack woke first and shook Jimmy. "We're here, bro, and you're staying for the day. No arguments."

Now, normally Jimmy wouldn't want to be staying for this family thing; he'd rather hang out with the band. The poor boy just wasn't much on domestic events (I'll tell you more about that soon), even if the family belonged to his brother's girlfriend, Kara, who was his childhood next-door neighbor. But the one thing that can change a man's mind made Jimmy stay—the love of a woman. Kara's best friend,

Charlotte, would be here today, and Jimmy was falling in love with her. He'd known Charlotte briefly as a child, and he denied this blooming love to his brother and anyone who would listen. No one believed him. Love like that is obvious to everyone within a heart's distance.

"We have to be on the road by 9:00 a.m. for the concert in Nashville," Isabelle, one of the backup singers, called from the back of the bus, her voice still as brittle and hard as it had been since Jack admitted his love for Kara. She couldn't help it—love denied sometimes hardens the heart. It doesn't have to be this way, and Isabelle's heart will soften with time.

Jack and Jimmy stood at the bus door when Porter Larson, Kara's dad, appeared and poked his head into the bus. He hugged Jack. Now, this right here was a Thanksgiving miracle because Mr. Larson was none too keen on Kara's breaking up with Mr. Hotshot Golfer to hook up with an old neighbor who was now in a country band. But Porter's smile and hug sang of a changed heart.

"Hello there!" Porter hollered, uncomfortable around the band, but wanting to be friendly. "What's everyone doing for Thanksgiving?" He glanced around the bus.

Isabelle answered for the group. "Happy Thanksgiving to you, Mr. Larson. I think we're headed to the beach for the afternoon. We have a concert tomorrow, so . . . "

"Oh, no, you don't," Porter said. "You're coming to spend the day with us."

Luke, the band director, stood up and walked toward the front of the bus. "We're fine, Mr. Larson. You've got your hands full with the Sullivan boys here."

"Please," Porter said. "We'd love it and we have plenty of food. Kara and Charlotte have been cooking for days."

The band members shrugged and laughed (except for Isabelle). Harry, the drummer, stood, holding drumsticks in his hand as he always did. He played the air when he couldn't play the drums. "I'm betting Kara Larson's turkey is better than our sub sandwiches."

The house was bright and warm that morning as the bedraggled group followed Mr. Larson to the living room. Jimmy burst through the door, hugging and greeting the entire family. The smell of cinnamon, pine, and something cooking in the back of the house filled Jimmy with a longing for things lost and never had. He wondered how he, so undeserving, could be blessed enough to walk into this house, into this family, and toward the open arms of Charlotte Carrington.

Then the noise began. Kara's sister and brother-in-law, Deidre and Bill, came through the front door at the same time, hollering for help with the food and case of wine. Then came Kara's brother, Brian.

The house filled with noise in that gorgeous way of family, of laughter and private jokes. The band crowded the living room, men and women with guitars and drumsticks looking misplaced on the prissy antique furniture of Mr. Larson's living room, which looked exactly the same as the day his wife, Margarite, passed away, twenty years ago. Damask curtains fell to the floor where Isabelle sat cross-legged, and she began to tell the stories, the ones about Jimmy and his antics on the road. She is good at this, and laughter rang out like the sound of hope as she told the story about Jimmy's hiring a girl to run up on stage and dance around Jack, trying to rope him with a lasso as he sang the Toby Keith song "Shoulda Been a Cowboy."

Jack shook his head. "I'm telling you, I almost killed him, but what would we do without Jimmy's jokes on tour? I think sometimes they save us from insanity, even when we beg him to stop." The combined voices and warm food, the cold wine and deep laughter, filled the room.

Sometimes Thanksgiving Day is all it should be in a family, in a home. That day inside the Larson home was one of those. In the simple and undeserved way of love, hearts mended and relationships were stitched together over food, twinkling lights, bad jokes, laughter, and melancholy memories. They talked about Maeve Mahoney, the Irish woman Kara believes brought her back to Jack. They spoke of Margarite and how both Margarite and Maeve seemed to be present in all that was said and done that day. They spoke of Jack and Jimmy's sweet mother, Andrea, now in California. Even Isabelle's mouth broke into a smile that didn't leave her face for the remainder of the day.

Charlotte brought her mother, Rosie, and soon the house filled with a light that Jimmy believed only he could see. He watched Charlotte with her wide smile and long blonde curls, Charlotte with her sweet laugh, tender touch and gentle words. Families had never been a safe place for Jimmy, and he'd believed they never would be, like growing up in a war-torn country and then believing that all lands are the same. But here he was beginning to relax into the rhythm of a new place where Charlotte inhabited not only the Lowcountry, but also his heart.

*C*harlotte and Jimmy met as all the best lovers do—when they weren't looking for love, when they were too busy to notice they'd stumbled upon treasure. They were brought back together when Kara and Jack reunited.

Now, Kara and Jack's love story has been told, but it is so beautiful that I love to tell it again and again, recalling the events with long, beautiful sighs.

You see, Jack and Kara were childhood sweethearts, yet were separated when they were twelve years old. You can split a boy and girl apart, but here's what you can't do: take the love out of their hearts. No, you just can't. Love is alive inside a heart the same way blood moves inside a body—running and thrumming through every cell and unseen thing that make us who we are.

The story of how they ended up together is much more complicated than just finding one another again. It had been in May of the previous year, and sweet Kara was engaged to the wrong man. Not a bad man. No, not that. Just wrong for her. Now, poor Kara had lost her mother when she was nine, and her daddy was a strict man who just wanted the best for his daughter and thought that her famous fiancé was the best thing for her. She wanted to please her daddy. Who doesn't? This is built into the human soul like a building block.

Kara was working for the PGA Tour, not only a grand job in her father's eyes but a vocation that allowed her to meet Peyton Ellers, who was and is a star on the tour. Peyton was all those things a girl like Kara, a good girl trying to do all the right things at the right time, would have looked for and loved. And sometimes when everything looks just right, we think it is just right when it merely looks that way. We have to search a little deeper.

About this time in Kara's very perfect life entered this batty old lady named Maeve Mahoney. Well, to be precise, Kara entered Maeve's life when Kara walked through the front doors of the Verandah Nursing Home and into Maeve's room, stating, "I'm here to spend some time with you."

You see, although Kara was "spending time" with Maeve, these times were "volunteer" hours mandated by the Service League, hours that Kara needed to fulfill in order to avoid being fined. Kara showed up with a pleasant-enough attitude, but yes, she was assigned to spend time with this woman. Maeve immediately saw that Kara was leafing through a wedding magazine, and that she was harried, hurried, and preoccupied, so Maeve began to speak about true love, narrating first-love stories. Now, let me tell you, Kara merely and only tolerated this woman's ramblings at first, believing that Maeve was crazy and had confused life and love and Ireland and Palmetto Pointe into a mishmash of memories. But soon it became evident that Maeve was telling a love story, one that sounded a lot like the tale of the Claddagh ring, a story clouded in myth and legend with a little blarney thrown in for good measure. Is there any better kind of story?

The Claddagh ring is that common symbol we all know—two hands circling a crowned heart—worn by lovers and friends all over the world. A symbol of love and fidelity. The tale goes something like this: There was a man from

Claddagh, Ireland, Richard Joyce. In the seventeenth century he left the woman he loved and sailed to the West Indies for a job, but alas, on the way, he was kidnapped by Moorish pirates and sold into slavery. Eventually, he apprenticed to a goldsmith in Algiers, where he fashioned and crafted the first Claddagh ring of gold as a gift for the woman he loved back home, the woman he knew he would return to one day. When Richard was finally freed, he came home and discovered that his true love had waited; he gave her the ring, and they wed. Ah, the perfect love story, right?

Well, soon the myth of Richard Joyce and Maeve's own love story about a man also named Richard began to weave into one love story until Kara was quite sure that Maeve was mixing up life and myth, confusing fact and story—Kara not yet knowing that all those can and often do combine into the most beautiful of all things: truth.

In broken fragments, Maeve told Kara of her own love, her own Richard, a man Maeve loved and lost and searched for and never found, a man who broke her heart and a man for whom she wished she'd had the tenacity and heart to have waited. This tender story opened Kara's heart to what she had known all along: She still loved Jack Sullivan. Yet and still, Kara did not believe that Maeve's story was "real," as the details were far too close to the myth of the Claddagh ring.

During these days that Kara came to love Maeve and her legends and tales, she also came to realize that in many ways Maeve was also telling Kara's story, asking Kara to look into her own heart to find the truth of her life. Soon Kara understood the lessons inside Maeve's narrative, and it was then and only then that Kara began to listen to the hints and proddings of her own heart. And it was then that she went to look for Jack Sullivan.

Kara spent hours listening to Maeve, pondering the questions Maeve asked her, questions like: "If you knew he'd return, would you wait for him?" and "Who was your first love?" Yet Kara still did not believe Richard was a real man until she found historical documents about the man Maeve had once loved, Richard O'Leary. Only then had Kara finally believed in the truth.

Who can tell the exact moment when a woman or man believes in something? Who can tell the exact moment when someone falls in love? Same thing. Believing. Love. Same thing.

So, you see, both Maeve's myth and truth brought Jack and Kara back together. And sometimes, oh, sometimes, it is this kind of love that also changes everything else in their world. Which this love did do.

I'm sorry—I know I digressed. Let me get back to how Jimmy and Charlotte came together because that is what this story of the song is all about. Well, really it's all about undeserved love, but the story of the song and undeserved love are one and the same. You'll see.

Charlotte is Kara's best friend and has been since second grade. Kara and Charlotte found each other during that time in life when a mother's death leaves a hollowed-out hole in the soul. Their common interest in art drew them together, although they could not have understood at that young age what brought them together; they merely felt that their hearts called out for one another in an immediate way.

The way an author wraps words around life to explain and describe, so Kara uses her camera and Charlotte her designs, both making sense of life through artistic expressions. And except for their deep love for one another, that is where their similarities end. Kara is organized and precise, whereas Charlotte is scattered and free-spirited; Kara's hair is a deep brown, straight and controlled, whereas Charlotte's loose blonde curls fall free and wild no matter what she tries to do with them. Kara's cottage is a home on the water, filled with white furniture and clean lines; Charlotte's apartment overflows with swatches of fabric, paint chips, and poster boards, toppling with ideas. Kara's books are in painted bookcases lined up alphabetically by author, Charlotte's books arranged in no order other than color and style.

Sometimes friendships form in the long flow of days, like a river carving a new path through the land, and yet other friendships are wrought together like iron to iron in a single moment. The day of Kara's mother's funeral, the adults, engulfed in their own grief, had left the girls alone for most of the day. Together they'd hidden under the branches and tangled roots of the old magnolia tree in the front yard. Curled into one another with ham sandwiches wrapped in flowered napkins, chocolate chip cookies melting in their pockets, they'd eaten, whispering stories of ghosts and angels, of where Margarite Larson was at that moment. Had she been able to talk to Jesus? After the devastation of chemotherapy, had all her hair grown back when they gave her a halo? They'd then fallen asleep to the lullaby of the wind, of the voices of adults wafting toward them, but never fully reaching their ears.

When the darkness settled into the crevices of the yard, and when the day they buried Kara's mother finally ended, no one could find the best friends. Adults called their names, searched the neighbors' homes and yards. Yet it was Jack who discovered them. It was Jack who knew where they'd gone and why. He slipped under the branches and woke them, knowing in that way that children know that the friends would not want anyone to see where they'd been. Together the three of them walked into the dark night, where Charlotte looked up to the brightest stars and said, "Do you think she can see us through those holes in the sky?"

"Those aren't holes, Charlotte," Kara said in a voice that was now more grown-up than it had been even a day before, death somehow transforming a child into an adult.

Charlotte stopped, grabbed her best friend's hand. "Tonight they can be holes in the sky, right?"

Kara stood for the longest time staring up into the sky and even past the sky, farther and deeper, until she returned her gaze to Charlotte and Jack. "Yes, well, yes, they could be holes if we wanted them to be."

And together the three friends slipped quietly into the house where the friendships that last forever tie their first knots into the soul. You see, there are moments, small and momentary, fleeting but defining, and Kara had decided right there, in that moment, on that night, that even with her mother gone, mystery still remained; with her best friend and Jack at her side, magic yet lingered.

And Jimmy, well, he is Jack's brother. And let me tell you something, these boys have suffered in this world. Oh, my heart aches to think of their hurt. The pain a father can inflict on his son I think is almost the worst pain there is. And love heals even that. Yes, love heals the worst of all pain. It is why Love is here in this world, why Love came unasked and undeserved.

So Jimmy and Charlotte were, as I said, forced together by circumstance, yet their hearts came together with something altogether different from mere situation. Which brings me back to the song.

*J*immy sat in the Larson living room, and if love can be overwhelming (which, of course, it can be, or it isn't love), it was at that moment. And this is what he thought when Charlotte walked across the room:

> *I cannot find or define the moment you entered*
>   *my heart.*
> *When you entered and turned a light on in the*
>   *deepest part.*

Lyrics began to form in his mind as Jimmy grabbed a notepad and pen from the kitchen, and then slipped away quietly to the footbridge at the end of the road. He glanced backward at the house next door to the Larsons', the house where he had grown up and left at sixteen years old. Yes, Jack and Jimmy grew up next door to Kara. The tangled memories often left Jimmy dizzy. How should he feel about a place where he had once had a mother as loving as his, a place that had allowed him to live in this quaint, coastal town, and yet a home where an abusive and drunk father hung like a noxious, poisonous cloud over their lives?

Only a woman like Charlotte could get him to return to this land and world to celebrate a holiday. Jimmy sat in the damp, quiet afternoon, the cicadas clicking the notes of the music, the river carrying lyrics, the air itself drenched with the song for Charlotte, the song about undeserved love entering a heart to change it forever. When he'd finished, he slipped the song into his back pocket and returned to the house, to Charlotte.

Now, Jimmy didn't want to sing this song to Charlotte until Christmas Day (it would be the only present he could afford). He wanted to polish and fix the words, make it perfect, although it had arrived complete as it was—the song, his secret.

When he returned to the house Charlotte stood in the kitchen washing dishes with Kara. There Charlotte stood with her blonde curls loose and tangled, the smell of soap and spice mixed into the warm kitchen, her voice soft and full. He came up behind her, kissed her ear.

She turned to his smile. "Where have you been?"

"I just needed some fresh air."

"We are all just too, too much sometimes, aren't we?" she asked, lifting her gloved and soapy hand.

"Yes," he said. "Sometimes." He laughed. I love when this man laughs because for so many years he was unable.

"I'm sorry," she said. "I know holidays are . . . not your favorite."

"No, not my favorite," he said. "But you are."

She shook her head. "Oh, Jimmy." She rested her head on his shoulder and sighed.

It is a blessed thing when a woman loves a man this way. It is where healing begins in a heart. Ah, but more must happen, because this was only the beginning.

CHAPTER TWO

Your story, your life, and your journey
all involve what came before you and
what comes after—all hints of who you are.

—Maeve Mahoney to Kara Larson

Exhausted, full, and sated, the band found their usual seats and dozed off as the bus headed toward Nashville.

Isabelle moaned. "I should not have had that last piece of pumpkin pie."

Jimmy moved to the backseat and watched his childhood home fade from view. He ran his finger along the edge of his new song. His love song. Although he'd been back to Palmetto Pointe a couple times since Jack and Kara started dating, the last time he'd seen his childhood home fade from view, he'd been in a wood-paneled station wagon with his sobbing mother driving away from a drunken man, a U-Haul trailing wobbly and unsure behind the car. The memory made him turn away from the window. It really didn't matter what things looked like now; he only saw what was then, back then.

Jimmy is the older brother, and he'd always felt like he should have been able to protect Jack and his mama from their drunken dad. Jimmy doesn't even like to use the word "dad," but he doesn't like to call him by his first name either, as if he knows this father, as if he is intimately connected enough to call his name out loud. Jimmy would prefer not to talk about or think about his dad in any way, but how can a human do that?

When Mrs. Sullivan, Jack, and Jimmy did finally escape the grip of Mr. Sullivan's whiskey breath and callous hands, they had to leave Kara behind. In simplest terms: They ran away. They packed a U-Haul and left Palmetto Pointe, and drove until Mrs. Sullivan, God bless her heart, couldn't drive anymore. The three of them landed in Texas, where the brothers grew up and fell in love with making music. Years later, their mother did finally make it to California, where she now lives.

Jimmy and Jack grew up not only as brothers but also as one another's father, one taking the place when the other needed it the most. Christmas, to Jimmy, was just another day, about as meaningful as the summer solstice or the Chinese New Year—something someone else somewhere celebrated.

One of the myriad ways these boys coped with their nomadic life and the sudden absence of a father was creating music. Now, you'd think that they'd have been thrilled to have a drunken, beat-them-up dad out of their lives, but in memory a dad is a dad, and a boy can miss the image of him more than he can miss the actual person.

Music became the thing between the brothers that a father could have been: a bond, a teacher, a feeling of something meaningful and wholesome.

Together, Jimmy and Jack wrote music, played music, talked about music. They essentially at some point began to live for the music. Their band, the Unknown Souls, is an up-and-coming sensation. Okay, I love them, so I'm exaggerating. They travel through the southern United States to get their name out there, opening for acts like Vince Gill and Martina McBride. Now, when I say "open," I mean the opening act before the opening act, and sometimes a song before the two opening acts.

In the music and lyrics they've found their way in the world. It's not how most people navigate a life, but it's theirs.

And it's enough. And until Jimmy met Charlotte, he believed the music would always be enough.

*J*immy didn't love her the first time he met her. It's not that kind of story. Charlotte was merely and only his brother's girlfriend's best friend, like an extra in a movie, or the minor character in a novel, not a real person at all. Cute, yes, but not real; a childhood memory. Charlotte was full of smiles and laughter, a tender, quiet luminosity in every corner of every room. But this isn't Jimmy's way—he is boisterous, loud, and funny in a take-up-the-air-in-the-room way. His light is more a blinding strike. Yes, both of them are light, but not the kind that notices the other right away.

They remet at a PGA Tour party where the Unknown Souls had played for a championship award ceremony. The party was silly to Jimmy—all these golf athletes milling around, talking about their latest championships, about scores and putts and birdies. Kara had been preoccupied with her job and her then fiancé (a golfer who had just lost the championship with one last putt). The band had left immediately after the party, Jack insistent on getting as far away from Kara as quickly as possible. Jack's heart was breaking, but he didn't want to face that fact and was flat-out angry. So Jimmy barely noticed Charlotte—he said hello, smiled. The End. Or so he thought.

Now, Charlotte might not be the first person you notice at a party, but by the end of the night, she might be the only one you remember. And this is what happened to Jimmy. Charlotte crossed his mind in the same way as a nice sunset or good meal, a gentle prodding.

Ah, but then months later, when Kara broke up with her fiancé and she and Jack reunited, Kara brought the brothers to her house for a cookout. Jimmy found himself alone on the back porch with Charlotte. Mr. Larson had been grilling steaks, and the air was resonant with spices and charcoal, as though the aroma had been embedded in the humidity like rain inside a cloud.

Charlotte stared out over the backyard where they could both see the white-shingled corner of Jimmy's old house. She nodded her head toward the house. "So you lived there when you were little."

"Yep," he said. "I did. I try not to think too much about it. Sometimes when I look at the house it seems like something out of a scrapbook, not really mine at all. We left when I was sixteen."

"I know," she said in this tender voice, almost like she

were singing a lullaby to a tired child, and then turned and smiled at him.

Now, when she did this, Jimmy felt something shift inside him, but he dismissed the feeling, thinking it was an odd emotion passing over him because of the house and all.

When he didn't smile in return, Charlotte put her hand over her mouth. "I'm sorry; I didn't mean to sound like a know-it-all. I just meant that Kara loved your mama. She loved when y'all lived there. I've been told so many stories—like about the time you rode your bike through the kitchen saying the brakes didn't work and you needed to hit something soft, which I believe was the couch. She says hanging out at your house was part of her best childhood years, what with her mama still being alive and you boys next door. She said you made her laugh all the time. That you were and are the funniest boy she's ever met."

Charlotte took a deep breath, and inside that small space—like the space between heartbeats—Jimmy let loose this gorgeous laugh. Charlotte thought he was making fun of her, and she turned away. He touched her arm. She looked over her shoulder. "I wasn't laughing at you," Jimmy said. "I was laughing with you."

"I was babbling. I do that sometimes. I wasn't laughing," she said, "so technically you weren't laughing with me."

"No, I wasn't. But the way you talk sounds exactly like you're laughing."

She smiled in that shy way.

Jimmy continued. "The brakes, of course, weren't broken. I just wanted to ride the bike through the house, and the back door was open, and . . . I did a wheelie over the top step, and then there I was coasting through the kitchen and into the living room."

What Jimmy didn't tell her was that his father then proceeded to smack him with a belt for getting mud on the living room carpet, for being an insolent boy who never had a lick of sense in his miserable head.

"Wow," Jimmy said staring off toward the house. "The bike story. I'd forgotten."

"We do that, don't we?" she asked.

"Do what?"

"Forget the good parts because we are so busy forgetting the bad parts."

And that was the end of that: Jimmy's heart opened wide, as if an earthquake had slipped the tectonic plates of his dismal childhood and moved them aside to let Charlotte's love inside.

Mr. Larson came outside and hollered for everyone to come inside for dinner. Charlotte walked away and left Jimmy standing there alone on the porch. It was then that he realized his hands were shaking and that he had this desperate need to run after her, after her joy.

We often don't know we've fallen in love until we look back and say, "Ah, that was the moment." This is how it was for Jimmy. He didn't know until he knew.

CHAPTER THREE

Your feet will bring you to
where your heart is.
—Old Irish proverb

The weeks between Thanksgiving when Jimmy wrote the song and Christmas passed in the hectic way of the world to-day. Times have changed. What was once meant to be a slow and calm remembrance of blessings, of our Lord's birth, of joy and family, has become a chaotic jumble of parties, over-spending, kinfolk drama, and obligatory giving. Oh, there I go, giving my opinion when I was just meant to tell this story.

For Charlotte, an interior designer, this is the busiest time of the year, what with everyone wanting to outdo everyone else with the most perfectly perfect Christmas decorations, as if it's about the lights, garlands, and yard art.

Some people know right away what they are supposed to do in life—others wander and stumble until they find their vocation and say, "Wow, I should have been doing this all along." Charlotte is the first kind. She knew when she was five years old that all she wanted to do was make the spaces in and around her life more beautiful. She made her mama crazy moving furniture and repainting her room every six months. She knew this town, the houses, and the women's tastes better than anyone ever had. This was her gift.

Now, if anyone can have two opposite experiences with Christmas, with life itself, it is Jimmy Sullivan and Charlotte Carrington. If you made a checklist and placed their lives one against the other, you would laugh and say that these two—Jimmy and Charlotte—would never even meet as adults, much less talk, much less fall in love.

Ahya, that right there is the absolute beauty of love: It just is what it is and shows up when it wants to show up. Unseen and unpredictable.

The week before Christmas, Charlotte and Kara stood in the Larson kitchen, baking their yearly Christmas cookies, which they put in tins and gave as gifts. This year they were also making shortbread in honor of Maeve Mahoney, adding it to the gift boxes they would give to friends and then distribute at the nursing home. Although Kara had moved out of the family home last year, this kitchen was much better equipped for so much baking.

Kara leaned against the counter. "So how are you doing with Jimmy being gone so much over the holidays? It's awful, isn't it?"

Charlotte wiped flour from her hands and picked up her mug of hot tea. "Yes, 'awful' would describe it. I don't know—I guess because I've never felt like this about anyone, it's awful and wonderful." She turned back to the cookies, plopped a silver ball onto a Christmas tree. "Missing someone you love is like nothing I've felt before. Everyone I've loved has always been here with me."

"I know," Kara said. "There is something comforting knowing that the man you love is doing what he loves, but it still . . . stinks."

Charlotte just nodded; she thought if she spoke, she'd cry.

The holiday season sometimes fills our hearts with unrealistic expectations, and the romantic visions of Jimmy sitting by the fire and telling Charlotte how much he loved her were in stark contrast to the quick and infrequent visits. Charlotte wanted him there to decorate the tree, to hang the lights, to go to all the parties and events. But he wasn't. He couldn't be.

Both Jack and Jimmy had promised to be home on Christmas Day, which Charlotte wanted to arrive much faster than it was.

"Only one more week," Kara said, filling her own heart with the reminder just as she filled Charlotte's.

"One week. And I have so much to do, hopefully it will make time go faster, but for some reason, I don't believe it will."

"Missing him will become part of every day, and it gets better. I promise."

Charlotte rolled dough onto the countertop. "I hope so. I really hope."

Yes, hope. What the holidays are all about.

*C*hristmas Day arrived as most days do: while we sleep. Yet Charlotte awoke at midnight, for no real reason at all (that she knows about anyway). She sat up in bed and then walked across the hardwood floor to the window. She stared into the dark night where the neighbors' multicolored Christmas lights blinked like frantic eyes. "Merry Christmas," she whispered to herself, to the world. She pictured Jimmy's bus moving down Highway 16 toward Palmetto Pointe, toward her, toward Christmas Day.

This was the only present she wanted that day—to see Jimmy. Little did she know that his present to her was more than anything she could have asked for. Charlotte crawled back into bed with a smile.

With family gathered in the warm Larson living room, there was a lull—a beautiful, syncopated beat between notes—after everyone had opened gifts and before dinner, and this is when Jack proposed to Kara in front of the family and the Christmas tree. Jimmy knew this would happen, and he'd waited all day, hoping for Jack to hurry so Jimmy could sneak off and sing Charlotte her song, so Charlotte would know Jimmy did have a gift for her, just not one she could unwrap.

After the hugs and tears, Kara lifted her glass. "I know it is love that brought us together, but I might not have had the courage to go looking for Jack Sullivan if Maeve Mahoney hadn't reminded me how authentic love feels, if she hadn't asked me this one question: 'Would you wait for him if you knew, if you really knew, he'd return to you?' When she asked me that, I knew, before I knew I knew, that of course I'd wait a lifetime if he were really returning. So instead of waiting, what did I do? I went to find him. So here's to Maeve Mahoney, her stories and her questions."

Overlapping voices shouted, "Hear! Hear!" as the glasses clanged together like heaven's wind chimes. The wedding talk began. Rosie and Charlotte talked one over the other with Kara and Deidre until the men—Porter, Brian, Jack, and Jimmy—slipped into the kitchen to collect appetizers and more champagne.

When they returned to the living room, Kara smiled. "Okay we think we have the best idea ever."

"And?" Jack took her hand.

"Ireland. Let's get married in Ireland at Maeve's church—that chapel she always talked about in Claddagh. Next year. This time. Christmas Day."

Jack smiled. "Perfect. Seriously perfect."

And as the details filled the warm conversation, Jimmy motioned for Charlotte to follow him to the back hall. He wanted to sing her his love song. He took her onto the back porch—the place love had grabbed his heart. He brought his guitar out of the case, strummed until he felt it was in tune. "Charlotte," he said, "someday I hope to buy you the most beautiful gift in the world, but today all I have for you is a song. I wrote it at Thanksgiving." There was a nervous edge to his words that Charlotte had never heard before.

She leaned forward and took his hand. "A song? Are you serious?"

He nodded. "There was this moment when you walked across the room and I was completely overwhelmed with love. Words filled my head, and I went down to the old footbridge at the end of the road. That's where I was when I disappeared for a while."

"I just thought you were exhausted of us." She smiled, trying not to cry before she even heard the words.

"So," he said, "this is my song to you." He played a few notes.

She put her hand on his to stop him for a moment. "What is it called?"

"'Undeserved.'"

And he sang. I believe the angels sang with him. No, I know the angels sang with him. And Charlotte cried silent tears that were the good kind of tears—ones of filling, not emptying. The family, who had snuck up and been listening the whole time, now burst through the door, and their private moment became a shared moment. And for the first time in Jimmy's life, he believed that Christmas just might be different from any other day.

∾

I'm not the biggest fan of New Year's Eve parties. It seems to be a night made for disappointment. All those songs and poems and parties about the new year, that big crystal ball falling in New York City and smaller balls falling all over other cities and other places, and people go putting so much stock into the night, as if the clock turning from 11:59 to 12:00 can change everything. This entire ruckus raises expectations to a level that just can't be fulfilled in anything but movies and books. I know, I know, it's the symbolism of a new year, a new start, and more than anyone you know, I believe in symbols, but it has become an extreme sport, this New Year's Eve–party thing.

All that getting drunk and finding someone to kiss and putting all that importance on resolutions and goals is just enough to make anyone depressed. And from what I can tell, this is mostly what happens on New Year's Eve—getting drunk and depressed. Ah, but maybe that's why everyone does all that silly drinking—to NOT think about the kissing and love and resolutions and goals. In my humble opinion (okay, so it's not so humble), New Year's Eve should arrive in humble quiet and glory. But that's just me.

On this particular New Year's Eve, Jimmy and Charlotte, along with Jack and Kara, went to a concert in Savannah. The Unknown Souls were part of a "Country Music

New Year" concert featuring all the up-and-coming country artists. And this is where it all began—where Jimmy's fame and therefore Jimmy's downfall began.

The Lowcountry coast during the holidays is one of the most tender and heart-opening scenes in the world. The lights set against the hanging Spanish moss and whitewashed porches look like angels gathered to sing. That year December arrived in a warm, moist nuzzle. The fancy scarves and hats, they were of no use. Soon January would come in with a freeze that broke all records, but for now there was a reprieve.

The holidays are beautiful anywhere they are celebrated, but they are extraordinary when celebrated in a place that honors the story. Not only the story of Christmas, but the story itself for just what it is.

What I also know—the stories change every year. The people who tell the stories don't know they change the details a bit every year until the story becomes a living, evolving thing. But here is the beautiful part: It is still the same story even if it sounds a little bit different each time it is told. The important part remains the important part. The essence stays. And this is what happened as Kara, Jack, Jimmy, and Charlotte drove to Savannah on New Year's Eve. Charlotte drove her convertible because they believed the warm weather would allow them to put the top down, but after twenty minutes on Highway 16 they decided it wasn't such a great idea. Charlotte's heart felt as if it were piled so high and sweet with love that it might burst.

She pulled the car to the side of the road, and Jimmy jumped out to pull the top up. Charlotte turned to the backseat and looked at Kara. "Remember that night your mama took us to see the Christmas lights in Savannah and she got a flat tire?"

Kara's eyes flashed with tears. "Yes. Oh, my gosh, yes. How do you remember that? We were like eight years old."

"And you wore a red taffeta dress with this huge green bow, and I wore this silly scratchy wool dress my grandma made for me that Mama forced me to wear so Grandma could see the pictures. And it was just the three of us—me, you, and your mama."

Kara leaned forward in the seat so she was in between the two front seats, her left leg and arm draped over Jack's leg. He didn't mind much. It seemed that every few minutes he was amazed again and again into realizing that this was his love. His Kara. Here was all he'd dreamt of during those years alone, during those years on the road. It was moments— common moments—like these that stunned him the most. Like waking up in the middle of a dream and realizing you didn't wake up but that it is your life. Just like that.

"And," Kara said, "Mama got out to change the tire. Remember? And it was freezing, and Christmas carols were on the radio."

"Yes." Charlotte raised her hands in the air. "And we were singing them so loudly that your mama came back to the window and asked if we were crying. She thought we were upset."

Kara laughed in that pure, deep way, and she looked at Jack. "Yeah, you know that and love me anyway, right? You know I can't sing."

Jack smiled but didn't answer. He just wanted to bask in this memory he hadn't lived but now got to relive.

Charlotte stopped, stared out the window. "And then that car stopped and helped us. It was an old man who didn't look like he could change his coat much less change a tire."

The top was up by now, and Jimmy climbed back into the car. Charlotte smiled at him. "We just remembered a time when Mrs. Larson took us to Savannah to see the Christmas lights and she got a flat tire."

Jimmy smiled. "God, I remember her in this hazy way where I swear I see a halo around her head."

"Thanks, Jimmy." Kara looked up to the roof of the car for a moment and then back to Charlotte. "So that old man changed the tire. Mama told him she could do it—that she knew how. But she was wearing this long black skirt and silver high heels. It was cold out. I remember the heat pumping in the car. But the old man said there was no way he would allow her to change that tire on the left front side because she would be standing up next to the traffic. He changed it in like one minute. It was weird. And then he just drove off without letting us pay or thank him."

Charlotte nodded as she started the engine. "We had the best night in Savannah. We saw every light and every house and even went on that carriage ride after we'd begged and begged. We drank so much hot chocolate that you got sick on the way home." She exhaled into the memory.

The car was silent as they—all four of them—slipped into that place of remembrance.

Yes, the essence of that story is true. Margarite Larson was a beautiful woman, but the facts? Well, they are all mixed up. Kara wore silver. Charlotte didn't even own that scratchy dress yet (she got it for Christmas that year). What is true—the old man. What they don't know is that he was sent to help. Even in hindsight we don't always see all the unseen forces at work in our lives. We aren't always meant to, I suppose. Sometimes help isn't given for recognition; it's just given.

Kara, Jack, Charlotte, and Jimmy arrived at the concert safely after passing an accident miles ahead of them, which had been caused by a drunk driver. They would have been involved in this wreck if they hadn't decided to put up the convertible top. Or maybe if they hadn't decided to put it down in the first place. Or we could go back even further—if they hadn't had to wait for Kara to run inside and grab her purse. There are so many things that work themselves into "chance."

The concert was beautiful. If you ever wonder what an angel sings like, listen to Alison Krauss. An angel's voice exactly.

The Unknown Souls were plopped directly in the middle of the concert, unfortunately in about the exact same place as an "intermission" might be in a play or opera. Sadly, the audience, unfamiliar with this band of extreme talent, used this opportunity to get a drink, visit the concession stand, or go to the filthy bathrooms. Those who did stay were talking or making out. Until Jimmy started singing his love song.

Ah, the hush that descended on the auditorium was almost holy. A quietude that caused breath to be held and eyes to open wide without blinking. It was a moment, well, many moments, when only the lyrics and music filled the place. A common man filling a common place with an uncommon beauty.

Kara and Charlotte were sitting backstage, sipping champagne and listening—they couldn't see the crowd, but when the quiet descended, they poked their heads out to make sure the stadium had not emptied. Charlotte's eyes— oh, the beauty of her eyes—when she realized that the song meant for her had filled others with the same bliss.

"They love it," Kara said.

Charlotte wiped at tears. "They do, don't they?"

Kara put her arm around her best friend's shoulder and squeezed.

Jimmy bowed to the applause and returned backstage to see Charlotte. "Hey, girl, they seem to like you." He kissed her in that soft way he has with her, as if she might break, as if she is the most fragile thing he's ever held.

She laughed, which is Jimmy's favorite thing about Charlotte. When she laughs he is filled with such delight he's unsure whether it's just too much—all this love is maybe, he sometimes thinks, just too, too much. That is what a man who hasn't had enough love would think.

"I don't think it's me they like," Charlotte said. "It's you. Your song."

"The song is about you." He kissed her and then held

her face in both his hands. "So if they like the song, they like you."

"They have no idea, but I'll believe you," she said, and cuddled up next to him, placed her fingers through his belt loops, and held fast.

This was the moment when the bald, stout, sweating man came running backstage. His name was Milton Bartholomew, and he was (and is) in charge of these concerts. A concert organizer. An expert in audience response. A man who knows when a song is destined to be a hit.

"Hey," he said to Jimmy, grabbing him by the forearm. "That song wasn't on the playlist."

Jimmy cringed. "Sorry. We substituted at the last minute. I just thought . . . Sorry."

Milton laughed so loud and long that his face was tinged with purple. "Whatcha apologizing for, son? It was brilliant. Truly brilliant. You wrote it about Christmas, didn't you? That's a Christmas song."

"Um . . . well, really I wrote it for my girlfriend." Jimmy held Charlotte's hand in the air.

"No, no, you didn't. You wrote it about Christmas. It's the perfect Christmas song."

"Huh?" Jimmy stared back at Milton, thinking that the man must have had way too much holiday cheer.

"The perfect Christmas song. All about undeserved love. All about letting that Love into your heart to change the world." Milton's hands were flying all over the place, as if he were throwing confetti or rose petals.

Jack stepped forward now.

You see there are moments in life when the smallest action leads to the biggest changes. We don't know—none of us—when those moments are happening. We understand only when we look to the past, and sometimes not even then. This was one of those moments.

"You're right," Jack said. "It could be the perfect Christmas song." He turned to his brother. "It's true. I didn't even realize it, but," Jack turned to Milton, "you're right. It is the absolutely perfect Christmas song."

Just then a famous country superstar, Rusk Corbin, walked by, searching for his guitar, and stopped to hear the end of the conversation. "What is?" he asked.

Now, at this moment everyone stopped and stared at Rusk. Jimmy and Jack didn't answer; Charlotte and Kara were starstruck, and Milton pulled out his cell phone.

Rusk tried again in that deep baritone voice of his that makes all hearts stop for a beat or two: "What's the perfect Christmas song?"

Milton then realized that the singer was talking, and he

covered the mouthpiece of his phone. "Hey, what's up, bro? Aren't you next?"

"I'm just looking for my backup guitar. Is someone going to answer me? What song is the perfect Christmas song?"

Kara found her voice first. "Did you just hear the last song?"

The country star shook his head. "Nope, I was back in the dressing room."

"Well, Jimmy here," Kara pulled Jimmy forward, "is the lead singer for the Unknown Souls, and he wrote and sang the most magical song of the night."

She stopped, embarrassed, realizing that this star was part of the evening's concert. "Well," she said, smiling her cutest smile, "so far, anyway."

"Can I hear it?" Rusk asked.

Milton stepped in now, placing his body between Kara and the star. "Ah, yes, you can. I'll get you a recording. But you, go . . . You're on."

"Happy New Year," the star said and was gone.

The foursome stared at him as he walked off, and then they all burst into laughter. They had no idea what had just been set in motion. No idea whatsoever. Do any of us ever know what's been set in motion when it is?

"It's almost midnight," Jimmy said.

Jack poured champagne into plastic flutes and handed them around. "This time next year we'll be married." He pulled Kara closer. "And we'll all be together in Ireland."

"Here's to next year. To Ireland," Jimmy said and raised his glass.

Ahya, the best-laid plans . . .

CHAPTER FOUR

*All of our lives we must choose between what
others define us to be and who we are meant to be.*
—MAEVE MAHONEY TO KARA LARSON

The year passed in the way most of our years do pass—with moments that stand out as memories and then with moments that seem insignificant (and aren't remembered) but somehow add up to a year. Marshside Mama's Restaurant and Bar was crammed past the fire-code regulations, but no one seemed to care, what with the bluegrass band playing and spring having blossomed in Palmetto Pointe like a full field of wildflowers. Springtime. Ah, the promise of newness it brings to everyone, bearing the smile of hope. My favorite kind of smile.

The crowd spilled outside and onto the patio where Kara and Charlotte sat at a round-top zinc table, leaning toward one another to discuss Kara's first big paying photo shoot in the morning. When Kara had quit her job on the PGA Tour, she'd fulfilled her dream of going to photography school and working in a studio. Now, finally, she had her first solo job. Night settled over the crowd, candles the only light futilely competing against the brilliant moon.

"Have you told Jack yet?" Charlotte leaned closer, her voice pressing against the other voices and music.

"No, I want to tell him in person," Kara said. "What other man would understand how it is to get paid for something you love and would do anyway?"

"Me. I'd understand," a voice said from behind.

Now, of course the girls recognized this voice immediately, yet they didn't turn; they waited for that brief moment where their eyes met and widened. Kara turned first. "Hey, Peyton," she said to her ex-fiancé.

"Hey, you." He hugged Kara, and she, in reflex, hugged him in return.

He stood there looking like the pictures Kara had once taken of him on the golf course—the absolute grand standard-bearer of the handsome athlete. Now, this is how he likes to view himself and how he presents himself. His gaze moved to Charlotte, and his face hardened into that false smile that goes only as far as the edge of his lips and no farther. "Hello, Charlotte."

"Hello, Peyton." She nodded at him, but didn't move from her seat to greet or hug him.

The awkward silence that comes with a girl seeing her ex-fiancé for the first time since breaking off the engagement filled the area, a silence that demanded someone speak, but no one knowing exactly what to say next.

"So, I wasn't eavesdropping," he said. "I was just walking past when I heard you say you got a big photography job." Peyton grabbed a bar stool from the adjacent table and sat next to Kara, actually in between Kara and Charlotte, turning his back to Charlotte.

Kara scooted her stool closer to the other side so Charlotte wasn't blocked. "Yes, I was hired to shoot an Easter family reunion next week."

"So, you really did it, huh? You really went back to photography school and left an entire career behind?"

Charlotte laughed in a sound that was much less like a laugh and much more like a cough. "You kidding me, Peyton? She left a job to start a career."

He leaned back in his stool and stared at Charlotte with his blue eyes, eyes that held a light that he could turn on and off at will. Here he turned the light off, leaving Charlotte to stare into blue ice. "I guess that would depend on what you'd call a job or a career, wouldn't it?"

Kara held up her hand. "Stop it, y'all."

Peyton saw it then: the engagement ring. He grabbed Kara's hand and pinched the diamond on either side. "Wow. So you're engaged already? Less than a year since we broke up? I guess I was right . . . " He exhaled and stared off into the crowd.

"Right about? . . ." Kara asked in the quietest voice.

"That it was someone else. That your little speech about not loving enough, or not knowing how to love me . . . it was a bunch of . . . " He didn't finish the sentence, but instead ran his hands through his hair, shaking his head.

"No, Peyton. That's not it. That's not entirely true." Kara lifted her hands in the air. "You know things weren't . . . right between us."

"Yeah, and now I know why." He leaned forward and placed his hand over hers, covering the ring. "Can I ask you a question? I mean, we were in love, or at least I was in love, so can I ask you a question?"

Kara nodded; Charlotte rolled her eyes.

"Is it that guy from the band? The guy you hired for the PGA concert?"

"Yes," Kara said. "But it's not the way you make it sound. I've known him since childhood. It's not like I picked up some band guy and let him put a ring on my finger. I've loved Jack since I was a kid."

Peyton shook his head in that motion a father uses when a child comes home with a bad report card, that kind of snarky shake of the head. "Yeah, okay."

Kara pulled her hand from under his. "Stop, okay? Let's not say hurtful things. It's good to see you. How are you?"

"I'm well. If you've kept up with my career, you'd see how well."

"I know how you're doing there," Kara said. "I meant how are *you*?"

"I'm okay. I guess this has been harder for me than it has been for you. It's taken me a while to get my feet back on the ground. I really thought we were *it* . . . you know? Really thought it was forever and if I just waited long enough . . . you'd realize it too, but here you are with a ring on your finger."

Charlotte stood now. "You know what? I think I'll go get us a couple drinks at the bar and be right back." She looked at Kara. "Okay?"

Kara's eyes widened. "I don't need another drink. So you can stay."

Charlotte took the hint and sat back down.

Peyton glanced between the two of them and then fixed his gaze again on Kara. "So, where is your fiancé?"

"He's on the road . . ." She looked at Charlotte. "Where are they tonight?"

"Memphis." Charlotte looked at her cell phone. "They should call soon."

"They?" Peyton asked.

"Well, Charlotte is dating Jack's brother, Jimmy."

"Now, isn't that nice for both of you? Two best friends. Two brothers. Yep, I'm sure that's true love, or is it just more convenient?" Peyton said.

"Stop." Charlotte's voice was hard, cold, not a voice she uses often. "Can't you just be happy for us, Peyton?"

"Happy for you? Sure. I'll try. I'll try as much as I can with a broken heart. But let me ask you this before I leave." He took Kara's hand and lifted it to his lips, kissed the inside of her palm. "Don't you miss me? Miss us? What we had? I mean, do you really want a life where your husband is gone all the time, singing songs on the road and being screamed at by young girls all over the country? Do you really want that life?"

Kara pulled her hand away, wiped her palm on her jeans. "Yes, I do. That is exactly the life I want."

Peyton stood. "Guess that's your choice."

"Yes," Kara said. "It is."

He looked down at her. "I still love you, Kara. If and when you discover that this is not what you want or need, I still love you." He walked away and toward a group of men at the far side of the patio.

"Let's get out of here," Charlotte said, raising her hand for the waitress to bring the check.

Kara shook her head. "It's fine. He doesn't bother me."

"God, he bothers me." Charlotte shivered.

Kara smiled. "You know, it just makes me understand how much I love Jack. There is this peaceful feeling that comes with loving the right person, a calm that I never had with Peyton, and it has nothing to do with what kind of life I do or don't want. It has everything to do with just loving. Just that."

"Just that." Charlotte smiled now also. "Exactly. I mean, if I look at it all rationally, loving a man who is gone most of the time isn't the best scenario."

"We can help a lot of things," Kara said, "but you can't tell a heart who to love or not love."

"No, you can't. But wouldn't life be easier if you could?"

"But not nearly as much fun."

Their laughter blended into the evening, into the music and into the night.

∞

$\mathscr{T}$wo weeks later, the brothers returned to Palmetto Pointe. Now, there are firsts for everything in a relationship: first kiss; first "I love you"; first fight. Well, this was Charlotte and Jimmy's first big disagreement. There must always be one, and this was theirs.

In the Palmetto Pointe Bridal Boutique, Charlotte waited in a room washed in white fabrics, couches, curtains, and wedding paraphernalia. Kara poked her head out from behind the dressing-room curtain. "Okay, if I come out, you have to be honest," she said.

"I always am," Charlotte said.

"Yes, fortunately or unfortunately, you are." Kara opened the curtain and walked out in her mother's wedding dress, a simple satin sheath that gathered under the breast in a crisscross pattern of crystals and pearls. The fabric hung to the floor, cream poured from a pitcher, flowing to the ground in ripples. "Is it too . . . old-fashioned?" Kara asked.

Charlotte shook her head. "God, no. It is so beautiful, Kara." Charlotte couldn't help but remember the last wedding dress fitting when Kara had emerged wearing an elaborate wedding dress that had looked like a chandelier, and she had, for the first time in a decade, spoken Jack's name when she should have been speaking Peyton's.

Kara twirled around. "Mama was a little smaller than I am, so we had to add some fabric in the back." She turned to display a panel of fabric that had been sewn into the back of the dress to look like a corset, pearl buttons in a line like bridesmaids waiting to walk down an aisle.

"I'm not sure this dress could be any more beautiful," Charlotte said, curling her legs underneath her on the white slip-covered couch.

A commotion began in the outer part of the store, laughter filtering into the fitting room.

"I know that voice," Kara said. "Don't you dare let him back here." She ran back into the curtained area.

Jimmy's voice first, always first and always loudest, burst into the room, Jimmy in his blue jeans and black T-shirt, his unshaven face and booming voice entering a bridal fitting room. "Okay," he said as he loped toward Charlotte. "There is my girl." He picked her up, twirling her around, squeezing her until she gently bit his ear.

"Put me down," she said, and then took his face in both her hands and kissed him the way you kiss a man you love and haven't seen in two weeks.

Kara poked her head out from behind the curtain. "Okay, y'all get out of here. And you," she pointed to Jimmy, "are not allowed to see my dress. Go."

"That's only the groom who can't see the dress. Me? I'm just the brother." He took two large steps toward the dressing room and pretended he would fling the curtain aside, but didn't. He turned and smiled that smile—that one that makes her heart flip over—at Charlotte.

She moved toward him and wrapped her arms around him. "Go. We'll meet you guys in an hour at Marshside Mama's, okay? I can't believe I'm saying this, but go." She made a shooing gesture with her hands.

He kissed her one more time and then left.

"It's safe to come out," Charlotte said to Kara.

Kara emerged from the dressing room fully changed into her jeans and white linen shirt. "Come on. Let's go."

"Wow, that was quick." Charlotte laughed and grabbed her purse from the couch. "Yes, let's go." Together they ran out of the bridal shop to catch up with Jimmy and Jack before they climbed into their pickup truck.

"Wait on us!" Kara hollered as Jack stuck the key into the driver's side door.

Jack smiled as he faced Kara. "Hey, baby," he said and held his fiancée. "You know how hard it was not to peek and see you in that dress?"

"Thanks for waiting," she said, kissing him. "I'm starving. Let's go get something to eat. I want to tell you all about my photo shoot last week."

‿∞‿

*M*arshside Mama's didn't have an empty table, and the foursome ended up at the long bar, hollering up and down, voices overlapping as the friends tried to catch up on two weeks' worth of stories and words.

"Charlotte," Jack said, leaning forward, "you should have seen the crowd waiting for Jimmy's autograph outside the bar last Wednesday. Here we are in Nowhere, Virginia, and Jimmy closes with your song, and the next thing we know—girls everywhere."

Charlotte tried to smile, but you could see the shake at the edge of her lips. "I'd line up for him any day," she said.

"They all think they're in love. It's so ridiculous." Jack took Kara's hand and kissed it. "As if that's love—seeing a guy onstage and thinking it's the real deal." He rolled his eyes and then turned to Kara to hear about her photo shoot.

Charlotte looked at Jimmy, and he smiled at her. "He's exaggerating," Jimmy said.

"Oh, it's okay if he's not." Charlotte took his hand.

"Hey," he said. "Let's get out of here, take a walk. I want my girl to myself for a while."

With a wave over the shoulder to Kara, Jimmy and Charlotte left the restaurant, strolling down the long dock to the water's edge. Summer hinted at the edge of these May days, a sigh of soft humidity sifting itself into the air, clinging to the skin like the closest lover. Together they sat at the dock's edge, their feet swinging over the incoming tide, an osprey flailing overhead, fighting to hang onto a fish.

Jimmy took her hand. "God, I'm so glad to be home. Tell me about the Carson job. Has she let up on you at all?"

They caught up on the facts and figures of a life lived apart, and then Charlotte rested her head on his shoulder. "You know, I understand why all those girls line up for you. I just hate it."

"Seriously, Jack was totally exaggerating."

"But how do we know, I mean really know, if this is love or infatuation? I mean, how do you tell the difference?"

He lifted her head off his shoulder and placed his fingers under her chin, looking her in the eyes. "Are you serious? You can't tell the difference with us?"

"Of course I can. I'm just asking how do you think *you* can tell the difference? I mean, how would you define it?"

"I don't know, Charlotte. I don't know if love can be defined. Can it?"

She shrugged and placed her head back on his shoulder. "Whatever it is, this is it."

"I don't think we have to find a *Webster's* definition to know it is what it is."

They were quiet for a time, one breathing in while

the other breathed out until Jimmy said, "Can I ask you something?"

"Mmmm . . . ," she said as an affirmative answer.

"Jack heard that Kara was with Peyton while we were gone. That the three of y'all were together in the bar one night. Is that true? Say it's not."

"It's true," she said and lifted her head. "But not that way. He found us here and sat down to tell Kara she was making the wrong choice with her life. It was silly and stupid."

"What else did he say?"

"Do you really want to hear this? It's ridiculous."

He nodded.

Charlotte let out a long exhalation. "He asked Kara if she really wanted this life—this life where her man was gone all the time. He said that the only reason we were all together was that it was convenient to have two best friends and two brothers dating. He inferred that she'd have a better life with him. After his tirade, he left quickly."

"Not from what I heard."

Charlotte lifted her eyebrows. "What do you mean?"

"I mean, I don't think it was quick."

"Well, it seemed interminable to me, but it couldn't have been more than a few minutes really."

"Oh," Jimmy said, but his voice held doubt the way a shot glass holds whiskey.

"You don't believe me?"

"I think sometimes we protect our friends."

"That's not what I'm doing, Jimmy. It really was stupid, and he embarrassed himself. So, I'm supposed to believe that all those girls who flock around you are an exaggeration, but you won't believe me about this?"

He looked away, and here was that moment where the past reaches up and behind a person and makes them act in a way they wish they wouldn't, when what went before weaves itself into the present and messes it up like a bad stitch in a long, beautifully knitted scarf. "I didn't say I didn't believe you." He stood and left her sitting alone, looking up at him, wondering who he was and where the angry voice originated. "I just meant that we should always tell the truth."

"I am," she said, hurt and confused, her heart skipping beats.

"Maybe you're right. Maybe none of us knows the difference between love and infatuation. I think that's what you were trying to tell me anyway, that you don't really know what this is for you. That you're not sure if this isn't just 'convenient,' that this might not be the kind of life you want."

"No, that's not what I said. You're misunderstanding."

And like his father before him, Jimmy walked away from anything that would make him dig a little deeper, go a little further. "I think I just need some sleep. I'll try to catch up with you later," he said.

"Don't leave, Jimmy." She stood now, took his hand. "This is silly. You know I didn't mean that I don't know about us . . . "

He held up his hand. "Let's not make this worse. We won't say any words that make it worse. Let's just leave, okay?"

In silence they walked the long dock back toward the restaurant while Charlotte searched for the single moment where he could have possibly believed she didn't love him, that she was confused about her feelings. Jack and Kara met them on the front porch of the restaurant.

"Hey, bro," Jimmy said, "I've gotta catch some shut-eye. Wanna drop me off at a hotel?"

Charlotte looked at him. "Hotel? Why are you staying at a hotel?"

Jimmy shrugged. "I'll call you later." He kissed her on the cheek with a kiss that didn't resemble any kind of kiss he'd ever given her—cold and distant, as if he'd never kissed her before.

Jack glanced between Kara and Charlotte. "Okay, let's go. Kara, baby, I'll see you in about thirty minutes. I'll meet you at your cottage."

She nodded, but turned to her best friend as Jimmy walked off. "What happened?"

Tears overflowed the rims and edges of Charlotte's eyes, the tide filling the marsh. "I don't know. One minute we're talking about the difference between love and infatuation, and then he asked me about Peyton and you at the bar. Then all of a sudden he didn't believe anything. He thinks I'm not sure I love him or want this life with him."

Kara exhaled. "Yeah, Jack asked me about Peyton also, but when I told him the story, he understood. I guess it's just a brother's protection." Kara sat on a bench and motioned for Charlotte to join her. "Listen, their history is complicated; I know you know that. But Jimmy has always felt responsible for Jack—as if anything that goes wrong with or for Jack is his fault. They had the most horrible father you could imagine. I know Jimmy doesn't talk much about it, but it still influences his mind and thoughts. Just give him a little bit to cool down. He'll see . . . "

"Maybe, though, he's right. Maybe I'm not sure if this is love or infatuation. Maybe he saw that in me. He's just gone so much, and then every time he returns it takes another day or two to get back into some comfortable way . . . and then he's gone again."

"I know," Kara said, also knowing that sometimes there

are no words to fix a situation, that sometimes a friend just wants to hear "I know."

*C*harlotte rearranged the swatches on Mrs. Carson's design board, attempting to focus on her work, on color and scheme and cushions, avoiding thoughts about Jimmy. But that's the thing with trying not to dwell on someone: The harder you try *not* to think about them, the more you do. A sad fact.

She turned up her Norah Jones CD and then poured a glass of wine. Maybe this wasn't the kind of life she wanted; Peyton, unfortunately, may have been correct. Waiting for a man who was constantly surrounded by other women, waiting for a man who wouldn't be there, wasn't the best way to live.

She sat down on the couch, unable any longer to focus on the demanding Carson job. She had just flicked on the TV when her cell phone rang. She glanced down: JS. She answered. "Hey."

"I'm an idiot," Jimmy said without preamble. "I just am. Will you even see or talk to me?"

"Of course I'll talk to you," she said.

"Well, good, then let me in. I'm outside."

She dropped the cell phone without hanging up and opened her front door to his beautiful face. He hugged her and then followed her into the living room, where she poured him a glass of wine. They sat facing one another across the dining room table; he pushed aside the fabric swatches and reached for her hand. "Charlotte, I am so sorry. I know you weren't lying. There is just this thing in me that sometimes rises up in defense of my brother, and then I lose sight of everything else. I am so, so sorry I walked away. That is what I should never do, and something I promise I won't do again."

She nodded.

"But can I ask you—do you think this is love, or do you think it's some kind of convenient infatuation?"

"I love you, Jimmy Sullivan," she said, her voice sure and steady. "No, I don't know how to define what that is. But then again I don't know how to define a lot of miraculous things. I do know that as I sat here trying to talk myself out of loving you, I only loved you more."

Jimmy stood and walked around the table, took her hand for her to stand, and then he held her. "I love you too, Charlotte. I just do."

And without a definition of love, love is still confessed.

CHAPTER FIVE

*Before he left he told me he loved me and
would come back for me. And I knew he would.*

—MAEVE MAHONEY TELLING HER STORY TO KARA LARSON

By the end of May, when the tides were higher than normal and the summer crowd was beginning to arrive and clog the streets of Palmetto Pointe, the phone call came in for Jimmy. *The Call.* It was Milton Bartholomew, calling to ask if Jimmy would please consider being part of Rusk and Hope Corbins' Christmas tour.

Jimmy, not quite used to getting good news, was confused at first. "Huh?" he asked into the phone.

"It's Milton. Can't you hear me?"

"I can hear you fine, but I'm on the tour bus, and it's loud. Now, what? You want us to do that Holiday Jam thing again?"

"No, Jimmy. This is bigger. Much, much bigger. This is the world's biggest country duo. They do a Christmas-concert tour every year, and this year they'd like you to open the concert with your perfect Christmas song. That one."

"Um, Milton, man, I think you got me mixed up with someone else. I don't have a Christmas song."

"Yes, you do."

Silence echoed back and forth between the phone lines as Jimmy searched his mind for some type of Christmas song. "Jingle Bells." "Silent Night." "Rockin' Around the Christmas Tree." What was Milton talking about? Jimmy didn't want to seem the idiot, but by God, he had no idea what to say at this point. Jimmy waited in silence.

Milton coughed. "'Undeserved.'"

Jimmy's mind reeled backward five months to the New Year's Eve concert, to the single comment about the perfect Christmas song.

"Oh, oh, that song. Yes."

"Yes, we are going to rename the song. Rusk heard the recording and wants to call it 'Christmas Love.'"

Jimmy's reaction was gut level—the kind that comes

when we know we're right and we aren't going to bend. "No," Jimmy said. "It's called 'Undeserved.'"

Milton laughed. "I don't think you get it. This married duo—Rusk and Hope—is the most well-known country-powerhouse married couple in the business, and they're asking you to go on one of the most popular Christmas tours in the country with the Nashville Symphony. You're being asked to join to sing this song. They want to open the concert with this love song to Christmas."

"I get it. I think. But we don't change the name of the song to make it something . . . else. It is what it is. A song about undeserved love."

Milton made a noise that sounded somewhere between a snort and a laugh. "I'll tell them you're in. Then we can negotiate the name."

"What exactly does 'in' mean."

"Fame. Adoration. Money."

"Milton, that's not what I meant. Dates. Concerts. My band?"

"It's not your band. It's just you."

"Dude," Jimmy said and stopped, glancing around the bus, "me and my band—we're one and the same."

"Not for this, you aren't. What it means is this: Fifteen concerts across the country. You travel in the band bus—not with the stars. Starts November 27 and ends December 23 in Orlando." Milton rattled off the names of some cities from Atlanta to Nashville to Sarasota. Then he told Jimmy the amount of money he would make for singing this one opening song.

Jimmy drew in a quick breath and looked at his brother, who was sleeping in the bus seat next to him, his head back and his face peaceful. This money could buy them a new bus, new instruments, and a few other luxuries they'd been forgoing.

"I have to be in Ireland by the twenty-fourth," he told Milton.

"No problem. There's a meeting in Nashville in two weeks. I'll e-mail you the information."

"Okay," Jimmy said, but he spoke to an empty line because Milton had hung up; when Milton was done, he was done.

Jimmy spent an hour staring at the highway landscape streaming out the window like a river of his private world. He was accustomed to this view—highway stripes, rest-stops signs, smaller cars buzzing by, thin, tall pine trees lining the eight-lane like sentinels of the southern highway life. He could be anywhere, but the view around the bus never changed. And he loved this—that no matter where he was or how far they traveled, the view *inside* the bus never changed: Jack. Isabelle. Luke. Harry. There hadn't been a lot in Jimmy's life that was familiar or stable, and when he found solid grounding—a home of sorts, in that bus with those people—it was enough.

How, he thought, could he possibly leave this band, his family, for a solo gig? But he'd said yes, hadn't he?

He needed to talk to Charlotte. There were moments when Jimmy was overcome with something miraculous in beauty or devastating in sadness, and both of these, as disparate as they seem, caused him to turn to Charlotte. This might be one of my favorite descriptions of love—this need to turn toward the one person who matters the most. Bobby, the guitar player, once asked Jimmy how he really knew he was in love with Charlotte, *really knew*. Jimmy thought for a long while and said this: "She's the one I reach for first." He'd finally found his definition of love.

Jimmy took out his cell phone and, taking a quick, guilty look at his brother, moved to the back of the bus to call Charlotte.

She answered immediately. She hates when he's on the road. Always worrying about him, always wondering and missing him in that deep-ache way. "Hey, you," she said.

"Hey, baby," he whispered. "Can you hear me?"

"Yep," she said. "Is everyone else asleep?" She'd learned the bus routine—grab sleep when and if you can.

"I just got the strangest phone call," he said, staring out the window to see Exit 14; they were now four hours from Palmetto Pointe. He knew almost every landmark that led from anywhere to Palmetto Pointe and how many miles stretched between that landmark and Charlotte.

"From who?" she asked.

"Remember that concert organizer, the one from last New Year's Eve?"

"Of course."

Jimmy recited his entire conversation with Milton about the holiday tour. Silence filled the line, and he though maybe he'd lost connection. "You there?" he asked Charlotte.

"I am. I am. I don't know what to say—this is so amazing. Really amazing. Your song will be known everywhere."

"Correction. Your song."

"You know what I mean, Jimmy. You wrote it. You sing it. It's yours."

"But see, that's the thing. It's not really mine. It's all yours. Everything about it is yours. And I don't know if I want them to make it into something else entirely."

"They can make it what they want," she said. "We'll know what it really is."

"Yes," he said. "Yes, we will."

"How far away now? Please say you're almost home."

Home.

Jimmy let the word echo through his body and heart. Home. He never, ever thought he'd again call Palmetto Pointe by that name.

That's the thing of love: Things we never thought would or could happen, do.

"Four hours," he said. "I'll see you soon."

"I love you," she said.

"And I love you."

Jimmy hung up the phone and dropped his head against the window, closing his eyes while the bus rolled toward Palmetto Pointe. Toward the love he now believed he'd never lose.

But here's the thing of it—we can all lose the most precious things in our lives if or when we forget their very value.

The whisper of summer heat filtered through the cool May breeze. Jack, Kara, Jimmy, and Charlotte spread a picnic across the sand of the deserted barrier island, sitting on blankets and towels. Now, at a time like this on a beach, the sun warming the hearts and minds, the dolphins nosing around, the holidays seem to not exist at all, so far away they are. But we move—in every moment—toward the future, whether we think about it or not.

Jimmy had all but fallen asleep on the blanket, that half-sleep that allows one to listen but not participate. Charlotte's voice drifted over him.

"Has Jack told you about the holiday tour?" She was talking to Kara.

Jimmy's sleep burst open to consciousness. He sat bolt upright. "Charlotte," he said. She sat next to him, her leg entwined with his like roots of a tree, their feet touching.

"What?" She turned away from Kara, who leaned back on her elbows.

"I haven't . . . yet . . . "

"Oh." She covered her mouth with her pretty little hand, which is something she does when she feels that she's talked too much or told too much or said something stupid.

"You haven't what?" Jack stood and then walked across the sand to the cooler.

"I wanted to talk to y'all about something," Jimmy said.

"Oh?" Jack asked, lifting the top to the cooler. "What is it?"

"Well, it just happened yesterday, and I haven't yet figured out what to do or how to say it. But here goes." Jimmy recited, again, the entire conversation with Milton.

Silence filled the afternoon. Well, not a real silence, but the quiet of nature: a splash, a seagull cry, a thick cricket-and-frog song, waves washing across the shattered shells in a sound that Jimmy had once written a song about titled "The Sea's Song of Broken Dreams."

Kara spoke first. "You'll be done in time to get to Ireland for the wedding, right?"

Charlotte laughed, but quietly as if in reverence for the question. "I knew that would be the first thing you asked."

Jack walked to the shoreline.

Jimmy turned to Charlotte, shrugged. "I'll be there, but maybe I shouldn't . . ."

Then Jack turned and faced the group, his face unreadable. "Jimmy, bro, I am so proud of you. I want to say the right thing right now, and I can't. I'm so proud."

Jimmy stood and walked to his brother's side. "You okay with this? I won't go if . . ."

Jack held his hand up. "You've got to be kidding me. Not go? I wouldn't allow it. You must go. This is . . . so right and good."

"But the band. They're gonna be pissed off. This will really mess up our holiday schedule. I mean—if I'm gone from end of November to end of December, we can't do a single holiday party or concert. That's lost money. But I've thought a lot about it, and I'll make enough money to give back the band double what they would've made with holiday gigs."

Jack reached into the cooler and pulled out the chilled bottle of wine that Kara had packed. He wasn't much of a wine drinker, but this moment deserved a toast. As much as the thought of not spending the holiday season with his brother almost broke Jack's heart, he was filled with proud pleasure.

Ah, the love when you care more for the other person's joy than you do your own. The real joy, not the kind that is meant to bring approval or love in return, but simple delight at another's happiness.

"It's done then," Jack said. "There is no more discussing it. You'll do it."

Kara stood now and walked to Jack's side. "This means you'll be home the entire holiday season. This means . . . ," she bit her lip, "you'll be here while we get ready for the wedding. You'll be . . . home." She exhaled the last word as if were the most beautiful word she'd ever spoken, and maybe it was.

Jack looked at her and pulled her close. "Yep. Right here. Sometimes things work out, don't they?"

Kara cringed when she realized that what meant a good thing for her meant loneliness for Charlotte. She looked to her best friend and smiled a sad smile.

Jimmy took Charlotte's hand. "You can come to every concert. I'll meet you in Ireland. It'll be okay. I promise."

"Of course I can't come to every concert, silly," Charlotte said. "But I'll come to whatever ones I can. And really, it's months away. Let's just have fun today." She kissed his palm. "I'm so proud of you. This is such a great opportunity. And yes, Ireland. We'll have that."

Kara clapped her hands together. "Speaking of—can we talk about it for one minute? I promise I won't be a Bridezilla and talk only about this wedding for the next six months, but I just want to ask y'all a couple quick questions. I desperately need your opinion."

"You so don't need my help," Charlotte said. "This is your expertise. Planning. It's what you were born to do."

Kara bent over and picked up a small gray-and-white-striped shell and threw it at Charlotte. "Thanks, pal."

"Hey!" Charlotte ducked, and then caught the shell in the air. "That was a compliment."

"Well, Jack and I really want to somehow honor Maeve Mahoney at the wedding. If it weren't for her, for her myth and her story, we wouldn't all be here today. There must be something we can do to honor her."

Jimmy dug his feet farther into the sand. "I think getting married in her hometown and using Claddagh rings for your wedding bands are more than enough. I mean . . ."

"Yeah," Kara sat down on the blanket and took a sip of wine from her plastic cup, "but those are more about me than they are about her. I mean, I want to go to Ireland. I want a Claddagh ring. I'm trying to think of something that is all about her, about her family and her story."

"Well," Charlotte said, "what meant the most to her?"

Kara stared out across the sea, trying to remember some of Maeve's words and advice. "I think she cared most about how story affects and opens our hearts. She cared about love and going all the way through a story. She believed in angels. She believed in love returning. Always this: love returning. She thought we all lived the same stories over and over at different edges of the sea. She didn't believe we should hold tightly to life, but keep our hands open."

"Yes, we honor all those things by the way we live, I think," Charlotte said.

Kara's eyes returned to the group. "I got it: her words. Last year I wrote down all the things she'd said and taught me. I can find something in there to put into the vows."

"Perfectly perfect," Charlotte said. "See, you didn't need me at all."

"Ahya," Kara said, imitating Maeve Mahoney, "I just needed you to listen."

And yes, sometimes that is all we need.

Charlotte rubbed her thumb across the concave dip of the shell that Kara had thrown, and then she slipped it into her beach bag. She never wanted to forget this day, this feeling of overwhelming love that was as profound as any love letter written.

We all hold onto things for memory; Charlotte would need this shell. Yes, she would—a reminder of love, both friendship and romantic.

CHAPTER SIX

For what cannot be cured, patience is best.

—OLD IRISH PROVERB

The trees were barren, and Jimmy spied a single leaf, shivering as if it were a living thing left alone in the frigid October wind by a cruel god. He was in Lexington, Kentucky, on a bench in an empty park. God, what he'd give to be in Palmetto Pointe.

Jack came and sat next to him, groaned. "That was the worst crowd last night."

Jimmy shook his head. "You call that a crowd?" he asked. "So, when does this stop being worth it? I mean, how long do we wait to break out before these gigs kill us?"

Jack shrugged. "I don't know, but I'm guessing we'll know by the end of your Christmas tour. If that doesn't start to change things, then we'll have to rethink all of this."

The iron bench felt like ice; Jimmy pulled his coat closer around his body, shoving his hands into his pockets. "Don't let the band hear you say that. And man, way to put the pressure on me." He smiled. "So if my perfect Christmas song isn't so perfect, then we're all done for good?" He shoved his elbow into his brother's ribs.

"Yeah, yeah. Poor you having to go out on the fancy Christmas tour."

"You know, I could ask if you can come and be my irreplaceable manager."

"Thanks, but no thanks. Carrying your bags while fans swoon all over you when I could be with Kara during the holiday season? Hmm . . . Let me think about that one."

Jimmy laughed that laugh that echoes into the sky, into the earth. "I got it. You've finally chosen the girl over me."

"I can recall a time or two when you chose the party over me. I won't have to think long or hard."

"Those days are long over, my bro."

"I talked to Mom yesterday."

"She okay?"

"She's great. But there's just no way for her to make the wedding. She's just too . . . frail . . . to travel that far. I told her not to worry about it, but of course she's worried. I assured her that we knew she'd be there in spirit."

A honk echoed across the empty park, and the brothers turned to see Isabelle standing on the bus steps, waving at them to hurry.

Jimmy waved back and looked at Jack. "All right, let's go."

Jack exhaled and stood, staring off into the winter day. "What city are we in?"

"Lexington."

"That's right. Lexington. Two more cities and then home."

They walked toward the bus, and Jimmy shook his head. "Who would've ever thought we'd call Palmetto Pointe home again?"

Who indeed?

Days and time moved forward until on a frigid November afternoon, Jack, Kara, and Charlotte said good-bye to Jimmy, waving as he climbed aboard the fanciest tour bus they'd ever seen—a house on wheels. Kara and Charlotte then spent their days preparing for the wedding, for the holidays, hoping against hope that the busyness would keep the loneliness at bay.

The sweet, sugary aroma of shortbread filled Kara's small white house. It was the week after Thanksgiving, and Charlotte burst through the front door and called Kara's name. She clapped her hands together, as the November cold had come early this year and Charlotte wasn't prepared, not even a coat did she wear. "I love this house," Charlotte called out. And she did. The whitewashed walls, the crooked floors, the single bedroom and bathroom, the galley kitchen with room enough for only the essentials, the whitewashed furniture that Kara had found in flea markets and antique marts, refusing family heirlooms when she was trying so hard to make her own way in the world.

Across the round, ancient pine kitchen tabletop Kara had spread photos of Christmas lights strung across various porches, trees, and lanterns. Charlotte walked over, leafed through the photos.

Kara came out of the kitchen, flour on her face and hands like a dusting of angels' wings. "Hey, you," she said.

"These," Charlotte said, pointing to the photos, "are amazing. What are you doing?"

Kara smiled. "I wanted to do a collection of Lowcountry Christmas lights. I took those pictures last year. Most are from around here, but some are from that trip to Savannah on New Year's Eve."

Charlotte picked up a photo of a gas lantern with the lights winding their way up the iron pole. "I think I love this one the most. What are you doing with them?"

Kara shrugged. "I think I'll add Irish ones after this trip and then . . . maybe next year . . . have a show?"

"Yes," Charlotte said. "Just yes." She nodded toward the kitchen. "Okay, I guess you started our gift tins without me?"

"You're only an hour late."

"Sorry. Jimmy was finally able to call, and I wanted to . . . catch up. He's in Atlanta. The Fox. It's so exciting for him I can hardly be sad, but somehow I am. I just miss him with this dull ache that won't go away."

Kara flinched. "This is hard for you. I know. I'm sorry."

"At least I'm crazy busy with work. Everyone wants the perfect Christmas decorations, like Christmas is a competitive sport and the neighbors' envy is the prize." She sighed. "And there's only three weeks left. What's three weeks?"

What indeed?

Jimmy stood backstage and looked out at the empty Fox Theater. He was awestruck by its lavish beauty. This theater built in the 1920s with a sky full of flickering stars and drifting clouds, a National Historic Landmark overflowing with artistic fantasy, was the place a singer rarely allowed himself to imagine performing, almost as if it were too much to dream, too much to ask.

He'd been in the theater only once, and that had been as a child and in the audience. His mama had brought her sons to see *The Nutcracker*. The brothers had whined and wriggled through half the performance, but finally the happiness on their mama's face and the stars above and the music had lulled both him and Jack into silence.

Rusk and Hope Corbin were warming up on the stage, doing microphone checks and playfully arguing about whether she should or shouldn't take her shoes off halfway through the performance (which she had the night before). Watching this in-love and married couple filled Jimmy with hope, but also with a deep sadness. These two were so adoring, and this intimacy made the tour a beautiful celebration of Christmas and love. And yet . . . and yet . . . it made him acutely aware of Charlotte's absence.

This was only their second concert, so Jimmy didn't yet have many friends in the band, and the loneliness felt like an emptiness, as if someone had come in and scooped out the middle part of his heart and told him he could have it back in a month. He was used to spending time with his own band—knowing every nuance, private joke, and hidden agenda—and here in this new environment he was just another guy. A guy singing one song.

A backup singer, he thought her name was Ellie, came up beside him. "Hey," she said. "Isn't this the most gorgeous theater ever?"

Jimmy looked at her. She was young. Her black hair was pulled into a headband, her face clean and waiting for the makeup artist. "It's beautiful. Really beautiful. Like it's not real. A movie or something," Jimmy said.

She laughed. "Okay, that's why you're the songwriter and I'm just the singer."

"What?"

Her hands flew through the air. "I said it was gorgeous, and then you almost made it into a poem." She exhaled and shook her head. "I've always wanted to write a song, but after hearing your song last night, I know there is no way I could ever write something like that."

"Of course you could," Jimmy said, feeling like he was encouraging a child.

"Hey, listen. There are a bunch of us going out after the concert. The Vortex. Wanna come?"

"Sure," Jimmy said. "I'd love to join y'all."

"Great," she said and ran off to the makeup chair.

Jimmy took out his phone and texted Charlotte. *I miss you. So very much I miss you. And I love you. xo.*

𝒯he concert went off without a hitch. Jimmy received his first standing ovation, and unscripted, the duo chatted on-stage about the beauty of the song, of undeserved love. Jimmy watched the audience, especially the children, enthralled with the wonder of the Christmas lights, the orchestra, the sweetness of the songs, and the soft sound of jingle bells playing in the background.

At the end of the concert, tinsel fell from the ceiling and across the stage, over the heads of the singers and the orchestra. Jimmy didn't know how they did it, but the duo and the orchestra feigned surprise when, of course, the tinsel falling was planned all along.

The curtain fell for the final time of the night, and Ellie stood next to Jimmy, pulling tinsel from her hair. "They love that," she said.

He smiled. "Yeah, so do I."

She shook her head. "You're a romantic, for sure."

"Me?" He laughed. "I don't think anyone has ever called me that. Other names, yes. Romantic? Not so much."

"Well, you are. That song. Liking the tinsel."

He shrugged. "Guess things change before you even know it."

She sighed. "I just think Christmas is so . . . forced. Everyone is working so hard to be happy. There are all these expectations for happiness and joy." She shrugged her shoulders, picked at her nails. "I'm glad to be on the road. How could anyone or anything be so happy and sweet for an entire month? I don't see how it can lead to anything but disappointment."

"I know," Jimmy said, swinging his guitar over his shoulder. "I've for the most part ignored Christmas. All this . . . cheer . . . is a little overwhelming."

"Exactly. It's like a magnifying glass—if you're happy, you're happier; if you're sad, you're sadder. And I think most are sad." She released a long sigh, staring over at the duo. "You think they could possibly be that happy all the time?" She nodded her head toward the couple laughing, his hand on her lower back.

"No way," Jimmy said, and then thought of Charlotte and the way he felt every minute he was with her. "Wait," he said. "I take that back. Yes, maybe they can. I think that yes, it is possible."

She shook her head. "I don't."

He smiled at her, feeling a little sorry that she didn't even believe in the possibility. Ellie walked off, and then called over her shoulder, "Meet us out back in twenty. Okay?"

"Okay!" he hollered after her. He realized, of course, that even a year and a half ago he would have answered Ellie with a more cynical tone, less believing in love and its ability to change his life. The difference a year can make, he thought. He plucked a few notes of his song and stared out into the empty hall. Even without a single person in it, the auditorium held a certain magic, a secret it wouldn't tell.

*T*he bar must have been breaking fire-code laws. People were jammed up against the bar and the tables. Flashing colored lights hung from the ceiling and walls. Patrons banged up against the fake tree where plastic Christmas balls rattled like empty hearts. The wrapped boxes beneath the white snow-sprayed tree were empty and squashed from the careless steps of those who crammed into the tiny space to hear the woman singer who looked as despondent as the holiday decorations. Men and women battled for one another's attention, hollering over the singer, flirting, buying drinks, and faking cheer.

This desperate grabbing for happiness never leads to anything but despair. Jimmy saw this and knew it also: the falseness that bears cynicism as its firstborn. He placed his beer on the bar and stood to leave.

Ellie grabbed his arm. "You leaving?"

He didn't want to scream over the singer, knowing better than anyone in the room what it felt like to be ignored while singing and playing an instrument.

"Don't go," she said. "Everyone wants to get to know you. Come on. Just a little longer."

"Okay," he said, knowing that he must travel and live with these same people for another month. It definitely wouldn't hurt to get to know them.

He sat back onto the stool, lifting his beer in a cheer as his answer. The band and backup singers, the grips and crew, began to motion from across the room—they'd secured a table. Ellie and Jimmy worked their way through the crowd, and Jimmy slid onto the bench, finding himself against the wall without a way to escape.

Within an hour he was comfortable—this was what he was accustomed to, this kind of nomadic life, this language of bands and singers and travel. He slipped with ease into the conversation and into the night.

Mickey, a crew member, sat across from Jimmy. "So, man," he said, lifting his drink to Jimmy, "you wrote that song for Christmas, and that's what got you on this tour?"

"I did write it," Jimmy said.

Ellie hollered into the conversation: "He didn't write it for Christmas, though. He wrote it for his girl."

"Really?" Mickey laughed. "I wouldn't be telling anyone that little tidbit. They're all calling it *the* Christmas song. The Perfect Christmas Song."

Jimmy laughed. "They can call it whatever they want as long as I get to sing it."

"I'm with you, man. This could be any concert they want it to be as long as I got me a job. I ain't complaining."

Jimmy nodded. "Exactly. I don't care what they call it as long as I get to play it."

Of course, that's not what Jimmy meant, but it's what he said, and soon the power of what we say changes what we mean.

The secret tempo of music and being on the road soothed Jimmy until he felt part of the group. The bar closed, and they walked out into the cold night, stomping their feet, clapping their hands, and walking toward the Fox, where the bus waited.

The bus lights brightened the side street, and they all stopped for a moment, waiting for the crosswalk sign to change.

"Home," one of the crew said, pointing to the bus.

"For now," another said.

They crossed the street, quiet, each one thinking of home and what home meant, where it was, and how they wouldn't be anywhere near it for three more weeks.

Charlotte turned the pillow over to find a cold spot and checked her cell phone one more time: She hadn't missed a call or text. She glanced at the digital clock: 2:00 a.m. Jimmy usually called to say good night, but something must have kept him tonight. She tried not to think too long or too hard about what that "thing" might have been.

She closed her eyes, but sleep still did not come. She finally stood and stared out her bedroom window. The sadness that arrives when one can't change a circumstance, when it just is what it is and there is nothing to be done about it, overcame Charlotte in the middle of the dark, moonless night.

The consolations she usually used to comfort herself— the reassurance that she'd see him in Ireland in a few weeks, that he loved her, that he missed her—weren't working this night. This is how love is between two souls: One can feel when something is amiss with the other. She knew, but didn't want to know, so she blamed the dark night, the loneliness, and the nonstop blinking lights across the street. She crawled back into bed and pulled the pillow over her head, sighing deeply into the sheets. "I miss you, Jimmy," she said. "Please come home."

CHAPTER SEVEN

The tongue ties knots the teeth cannot loosen.

—Old Irish proverb

*M*orning arrived quickly for Jimmy, as he'd been asleep for only three hours when the bus pulled out of the parking lot and headed toward Nashville for that evening's concert. He rolled over on his cot and groaned.

The curtain slid aside, and Milton stared at him. "Wake up, party boy. You're a star."

"Huh?" Jimmy rubbed his eyes, sat up too quickly, and banged his head on the top of the bunk. He swung his feet out and, rubbing his head, asked, "What are you talking about?"

Milton waved an *Atlanta Journal and Constitution* Sunday paper in his face. "You. Front page of the Arts section. All about the new rising star traveling with the Nashville Symphony and the famous country stars. But it's all about you. You."

Jimmy grabbed the paper from Milton. "Really?"

"Yep." Milton handed him a cup of coffee. "And you need to get your wits about you. I have more than seven magazine and newspaper interviews lined up for you today—all on the phone except for the live TV interview with *CMT Insider* at 4:00 this afternoon. So get your head together, get up, and let's get moving. Superstar."

"This is crazy," Jimmy mumbled, taking a very long swallow of coffee. "It's one song."

"One song. That's all it ever takes, son. One perfect song."

Charlotte awoke to the ringing cell phone and stared at the screen. She hadn't slept most of the night, and morning had come with a blinding headache. It was Sunday morning when she could sleep in. Who was calling?

She slipped her glasses on to see JS—his sweet initials. "Hey," her voice cracked on the line. She didn't understand her relief in hearing his voice, but relief there was.

"Hey, baby. Did I wake you?"

"Yes, but I'm glad you did. Where are you? How are you?"

"I'm somewhere on the highway, pulling out of downtown Atlanta and pointed toward Nashville."

"I wish I were there," she said.

"Oh, so do I." His voice cracked, and he leaned over the phone so no one else on the bus would hear him, although he knew they'd hear parts of the conversation. For all the supposed glamour of band and concert tours, there is absolutely zero privacy. He didn't used to care, but now he did. He wanted to pour out his loneliness, his deep need to see her. He wanted to holler about the newspaper article and the CMT interview. The feelings were piling up inside him like snowflakes, slowly, slowly, but insistently.

They were both silent for a moment, as if in reverence for the moment between them, the love and the aloneness that can never be cured with a phone call.

"I have some good news," he said.

"Tell me," she said and closed her eyes. "I'll pretend you're lying right here telling it to me."

He sighed. "They wrote an article about me. Front page of the Arts section in Atlanta, and now I have all these interviews lined up. I'm gonna be on CMT this afternoon at 4:00. Live. Watch it. They want me to sing the song. Your song."

"Oh, Jimmy," she said, and her heart filled in that way where words are never enough, where there just aren't any words to say at all because not one would be good enough or big enough.

The CMT Insider hostess, Meagan, sat on a stool in front of the camera while a makeup artist applied powder to her face, added eyeliner.

Jimmy stared at the studio as if he were in a dream. He had walked into the building wearing jeans and "The Unknown Souls" scripted across a black T-shirt. Within a minute, Milton's assistant had given him a plain black ribbed cotton shirt with two single buttons at the top and a gray cowboy hat. Jimmy slipped them both on and then looked at her. "I would never wear this."

"Today you will." She smiled at him and pushed down on the hat. "You look great. Seriously great. You're gonna break some hearts this afternoon singing that song, looking like this. Just smile and do your thing. You were made for this," she said. "Made for it."

Jimmy shook his head. "You might be going a bit overboard."

"I don't think so," she said. "Smile, now."

The producer made a motion for Jimmy to walk toward the couch where Meagan stood. He hooked a microphone on the T-shirt while rattling off directions. "Okay, this is live. So when Meagan starts to talk, look at her. Never look at the camera. You are talking to her and only her. When she casually asks you to sing the song, decline and then let her talk you into it. Then say, 'Okay, sure.' And then you'll have exactly two minutes to sing."

Jimmy lifted his arm to allow the tech to slip the microphone cord into his shirt and behind his back. "The song is three minutes long," Jimmy said.

"Then shorten it, dude."

Meagan stepped forward. "Hey, Jimmy. I'm Meagan. Listen, no worries about the length of the song—just sing it, and the camera will cut off for commercial while you're singing. It'll give them a taste without the entire song and sell tickets."

Jimmy held out his hand. "Nice to meet you. I'm a big fan of your show. It's a little surreal to have you interviewing me."

She smiled, motioned to the couch. "Sit and talk to me like we're sitting in my living room. Okay?"

He nodded and sat, but the cowboy hat was bugging him, pressing against his forehead, digging into his skin.

"Six seconds!" the tech hollered and moved behind the camera. He then counted down, and Meagan turned to Jimmy and smiled, nodded, mouthed, "Relax."

Jimmy smiled back at her. She turned to the camera. "Welcome back to *CMT's Insider New Talent.* This afternoon we are privileged to catch Jimmy Sullivan on his whirlwind Christmas tour with Rusk and Hope Corbin and the Nashville Symphony Orchestra. I know you might not have heard his name before, but after today, you won't be able to stop talking about him. I promise."

Meagan flashed her smile at the camera and then turned to Jimmy. "So, tell us, Jimmy Sullivan, how has it been traveling on this Christmas tour?"

"Amazing," he said. "A dream come true. The crowds have been enormous." He waved his hand in the air. "Now, I know those crowds aren't for me, but they're great anyway. I sing just one song, but for that one song, I can pretend they're all in their seats for me." When Meagan laughed, he was relieved, felt comfortable, and didn't think about what he did next—tipped his cowboy hat. He'd a little too literally taken her advice to make himself at home.

She laughed at and with him, leaning back. "Well,

then, Jimmy Sullivan, after we hear you sing I have a feeling that some of the crowd will be there for you."

"Ah," he said, now flustered, "I'm out there with Grammy and CMA Award winners. Rusk is in the Country Music Hall of Fame—I'm not kidding myself who the crowd is there to see. I'm just there to sing."

"We all want to know where you came from. Why haven't we yet heard from you before now?"

Jimmy smiled. "Guess y'all just didn't hear us in our neck of the woods out there in South Carolina."

"Is that where you're from?"

Jimmy shook his head. "Yes and no. We're from a little bit of all over. I grew up in Palmetto Pointe." He meant to continue, to talk about the band and Jack and Texas, but Meagan had other plans and interrupted him.

"Now, I understand that this song has been called 'The Perfect Christmas Song.'"

He laughed and leaned back into the pillows of the couch, threw his arm over the backrest, and flashed that grin that had caught Charlotte by surprise that night on the back deck. "I think maybe one person called it that, but it's nice to hear."

"No," she said, "I've heard this from several sources, and also from Rusk and Hope themselves. Can you tell us why you think it is being called that?"

Jimmy shrugged. "It's about undeserved love. The kind that comes into your world and takes you by surprise. The kind that opens your heart and changes your life. That kind."

"Exactly like Christmas," she said. "When love entered the world in an unexpected way and opened hearts, changed lives."

Jimmy nodded.

"Well, can we hear a little bit of it?"

Jimmy reached down and grabbed his guitar, strummed a couple chords, and then remembered he was supposed to resist, which seemed silly. "Absolutely," he said, standing up and moving toward the microphone they had pointed out to him earlier. As he walked toward it, the camera shifted back to Meagan.

"Here, live from Nashville, singer-songwriter Jimmy Sullivan singing his perfect Christmas song."

The camera swung toward Jimmy, and he opened the song:

> *I cannot find or define the moment you entered*
> *my heart.*
> *When you entered and turned a light on in the*
> *deepest part.*

Charlotte, Kara, and Jack huddled around the big-screen TV in Thomas's Pub with the remaining Unknown Souls. When Jimmy finished his song, the entire pub cheered and lifted glasses to Jimmy Sullivan—a hometown boy, they called him. Here's the thing: Anyone and everyone who's ever heard of Jimmy Sullivan will now say they were his best friend in second grade, or his girlfriend in fifth grade.

Isabelle was the only one not cheering, and Jack put his arm around her shoulder. "You okay?"

"He didn't mention the band or Charlotte or you or why he really wrote the song. He let them turn the song into something else. And what the hell was that cowboy hat all about?"

"Isabelle," Jack said, "it's just a two-minute interview. Don't get all tangled up about it. He's not deserting Charlotte or us. You know that."

"Do I?" She stood now, wrapped her coat around her body, and threw her scarf around her neck. "Listen, I gotta go. I'm wiped. I'll see y'all tomorrow."

Jack turned to Charlotte. "Pay her no mind. She's always been supersensitive about losing us. We're her only family."

The jukebox music blared now, and Kara leaned closer to Charlotte and Jack to be heard. "Yeah, she practically accosted me the first time I was ever on the tour bus. She asked me how I knew Jack, and told me I had no right to be there."

Jack laughed. "I don't think that's exactly what she said."

"Well, whatever she did say, that's what it sounded like."

Charlotte nodded at Jack and Kara, but bit the inside of her cheek. She didn't want to admit it, but she agreed with Isabelle. Jimmy hadn't mentioned any of them. He hadn't said whom the song was for or what the song was really about. She didn't want to be the "sensitive one." She didn't want to pout or whine because her boyfriend was just on Country Music Television and didn't say her name. But something deep inside her shifted, and she fought the rising tears.

"He looked cute, didn't he? Even in that silly cowboy hat, he looked adorable," Charlotte said.

"More than cute. Like a . . . star." Kara leaned into Jack. "This is really great, Charlotte. Really, really great."

"Yes," Charlotte said, wishing she meant it, wishing she really did think it was great.

Jimmy left the studio and walked into the cold Nashville afternoon. The setting sun bit into his eyes, the wind speaking in words he didn't understand as it whipped around the corners of the tall buildings. He was alone, and the victory of that interview didn't taste as sweet as it would if he had someone, just anyone, to share it with.

And that is the thing about wonderfulness or awfulness or anything at all, really—what is it if you can't share it?

Jimmy dug into his pocket, pulled out his paycheck. He walked down South Broadway, passing boot stores, bars, and restaurants. New bands and sultry-eyed singers wearing cowboy hats stared at him from bar posters taped crookedly to front windows. He stopped and stared into the front door of Tootsie's, where a band was setting up and a bouncer placed his stool at the front door, preparing for the evening.

"Hey," the bouncer said.

Jimmy nodded at him. "Who's singing tonight?"

"I'm not sure," he said, slipping his baseball cap on. "Want me to check?"

"That's okay. Just curious."

"They're all the same to me," the bouncer said. "Just another guy in another cowboy hat trying to get discovered. Singing songs about love and loss and broken trucks. The new ones all sing about being a country boy."

"Or about Christmas." Jimmy smiled at the bouncer, making fun of himself.

"Yeah, this time of year, that too. Christmas songs. Country Christmas songs about snow and being home and . . . Like I said, it's all the same to me. Just give me a decent guitarist, and I'm all good."

"I'm with you, man." Jimmy began to walk away and then turned back. "Hey, where's the closest jewelry store?"

"Two doors down on the right."

"Thanks," Jimmy said, knowing now exactly what to do. The bouncer was right—it was all the same. What made this fame any different? What made him different? What made the song different? Charlotte.

It was time to tell her the reason—the only reason he was now a different man.

The bell clanged as he pushed the heavy door to enter the store. A woman in all black with more jewelry than one person should wear together came to the glass counter. Jimmy glanced around the store at the gold necklaces and huge carved belt buckles, at the dangling earrings and gaudy rings made of gold and colored stones bigger than a golf ball.

The woman approached Jimmy. "May I help you?"

"Yes, I'm looking for an engagement ring."

She placed her hand over her heart. "Oh, this is my favorite. Finding engagement rings during the holiday season. You proposing on Christmas?" she asked.

Jimmy laughed. "Until about four seconds ago, I didn't even know I was proposing, so I haven't decided that part yet."

"Wow." She pointed to a case at the far side of the store. "Follow me."

Jimmy walked behind her until he stood over a case of at least fifty diamond rings. "Oh, I guess I should have given this more thought. I have no idea what I'm doing. I don't know anything about . . . this."

"That's why I'm here," she said, slipping a key from a chain and opening the case. She placed a black velvet tray full of rings on top of the counter. "Do you have a budget?"

"Yes," Jimmy said and quoted the exact amount on his first paycheck.

She smiled. "You sound firm."

"I am because I have to be," he said and smiled.

"Great. Well, here are the princess-cut solitaires. Or would you like oval or with baguettes?"

"Are you speaking English?" he asked, but smiled.

"Let's start here—tell me what you see on her hand."

"A diamond."

"All right. Anything more specific?"

Jimmy stared at the tray, the diamonds becoming one mass of glittering confusion. He closed his eyes and tried to picture Charlotte, where he'd ask, what it would mean to her. His eyes flew open. "Okay, I'll be proposing in Ireland over Christmas. Does that help?"

She laughed. "Yes, yes, it does." She reached inside the case and pulled out a single ring. "This is called a Claddagh ring."

Jimmy looked down at the platinum ring—the heart with the hands surrounding it, the crown above the heart, and a round, brilliant diamond set into the center of the heart. "Yes," he said, without knowing the word had formed itself and been spoken. He looked at the woman. "Yes, exactly yes."

CHAPTER EIGHT

*We live our stories over and over in every
generation, at the edge of every sea.*
—Maeve Mahoney to Kara Larson

harlotte stood at the entrance to the Verandah Nursing Home with Kara. This was the place where Maeve had once lived, where Kara's life had been changed by a single story. That is one of my favorite things about life changes—how they don't always occur in the place and space we think they should occur.

Charlotte placed her hand on Kara's arm before she opened the door. "You think Jimmy is okay?"

Kara released her hand from the doorknob, her other hand holding boxes of shortbread. Handmade garland was draped over Charlotte's forearm. Kara shivered. "Of course I do. Why do you ask?"

Charlotte shrugged. "You know he's never been alone on the road—he's always had Jack and the band."

"You talk to him every day, right?"

Charlotte nodded.

"And he seems fine?"

She nodded again.

"Then what's wrong?"

Charlotte fiddled with the garland. "I can't name it. I don't really know."

Kara brushed pine needles from Charlotte's hair. "You just miss him. It'll all be fine."

"Yeah." Charlotte forced a smile and opened the door to the nursing home. "You're right."

When the two of them entered the home, they were, as usual, overcome with the scent of disinfectant and baby powder. They walked back to the living room where the residents were watching *Miracle on Thirty-Fourth Street*.

Mrs. Anderson looked up from her puzzle and smiled at Kara and Charlotte. "Well, well, look who the cat drug in," she said with a lisp.

Charlotte looked at Kara and whispered, "I've never understood that saying—'what the cat drug in'? What does that mean?"

"I think it means that they didn't expect us."

The remaining residents turned. Some waved; others ignored them. Mr. Potter stood up in his walker and half-walked, half-rolled toward them. "Hello, ladies. I'm assuming you came to see me." He smoothed back the four hairs left on his head and winked.

"Well, I know I did. I'm just not sure about Kara here, what with her being engaged and all," Charlotte said.

Mr. Potter laughed and then spoke in that rough voice that told of his smoking years, of a scarred throat. "Well, what gives us this pleasure today?" he asked.

"We brought garland for the living room and a tin for each of you."

Mrs. Anderson looked up from her puzzle again. "What's in that tin? Did you ask permission from the front desk? I'm allergic to pine nuts, you know. And Dottie over there is a diabetic. And Frances, well, she can't eat anything that's been anywhere near shrimp."

Kara smiled. "It's shortbread. Just butter, sugar, and eggs."

Mrs. Anderson shook her head. "Now, how am I gonna watch my girlish figure if you're bringing me these treats?"

Kara placed the bag of tins on the table. "Well, you'll have to take that up with Maeve Mahoney. It's her recipe."

"Ohhh, you stole a family recipe?" Mrs. Anderson shook her finger at Kara.

"Borrowed," Kara said.

The nursing attendant entered the room and paused the movie. "Hi, ladies. You need any help?"

"I think we got it . . . but if you could just let me know if someone can't have shortbread . . . "

Soon the room was decorated as if Mrs. Claus had visited, and Kara and Charlotte walked out of the nursing home feeling fuller and stronger and more joyful than before they'd walked through the doors. This is how giving is. I know logic tells us that giving means having less, but that's not the way it is. Giving means having more. It's just the way it is. As Kara and Charlotte know.

The concert in Knoxville was sold out. Jimmy's nerves almost got the best of him, but he sang the song as if Charlotte were in the front row.

On this night he opted to stay in the bus while the band and crew went out. Sometime in the middle of the night he heard them come home, but his sleep was deep and silent.

Until the dream.

He walks out of a tour bus the size of a house, clouds low and dark. He pushes and yet can't move forward. Finally, he breaks free and attempts to walk toward the concert hall, yet obstacles are placed in his way— a gap in the sidewalk, a policeman not allowing him past, a wild fan grabbing at him. He pushes hard against it all, his head down, his muscles aching, his heart thumping to get to the concert hall, to the stage. Nothing else matters—not the crowd or the police or the gash in the earth, a gash big enough to swallow any man alive.

He awoke in a sweat, sitting bolt upright in bed. He felt he'd been sent a message, but not sure of what it was, he stretched back into his bed and closed his eyes.

He ignored that nagging sense of something important—ahya, one should never ignore that nagging sense. But he did. Oh, he did.

*T*here is this saying that time is relative. A very smart man said this, and it's true—it's all relative to what you want and when you want it. It seems to move slowly when you want something or someone, and it appears to fly at the speed of light when you're exactly where you want to be, doing exactly what you want to do with exactly whom you want to do it. There are also those times when it seems to stand still, to stop completely, as if time itself is holding its breath to see what will happen next.

Charlotte felt this way—that time was standing still. She looked at the calendar and counted the days until she'd see Jimmy, and yet the date never seemed to move closer. She kept track of his concerts and cities, but their conversations had dwindled from many times a day to almost every other day.

Her client, Mrs. McClintock, stood at the top of her staircase and spoke down to Charlotte—literally and figuratively: "Young lady, you promised there would be freeze-dried pomegranates on this garland, that you would add a splash of red." The woman fingered the top of the garland wrapped around the staircase and slowly descended the stairs, one deliberate step at a time, emphasizing each word with the click of her high heels.

Charlotte released a long sigh, smiling through her gritted teeth. "I explained on the phone yesterday that the supplier is out of pomegranates, so I used red berries instead. There is still a splash of red to accent the rest of your decorations."

Mrs. McClintock reached the bottom of the staircase, but remained one step above Charlotte. "Yes, but this is the exact same garland that Edith Carson has in her foyer. And don't try to tell me it's not because I was at her Christmas party last night, and it is the same. Now, what are we going to do about this? My party is tonight, and I cannot have the same exact decorations as Edith Carson. I just cannot. So, my dear, what are you going to do to rectify the situation?"

"Well," Charlotte said, "I can weave some dried oranges and then some magnolia leaves into the garland, and it will have a completely different look."

"Yes, 'different' is one word. 'Gaudy' might be another word. 'Cheesy' might be another. Oranges? Are you kidding me? My decorations are red and white."

Charlotte kept her smile. She wasn't sure how, but years of practice helped. "No one has white and silver antique balls. I have a box of the most fabulous vintage mercury ornaments in all sorts and sizes. You wouldn't be able to keep them, but no one, absolutely no one, will have anything like it. You'll be the only one. I was going to use them for the mayor's Christmas centerpiece, but if you want them, I'll give them to you and they'll never know the difference. Your garland will be the talk of the town. Forget pomegranates."

Mrs. McClintock finally smiled, and Charlotte knew she'd hit the right button—one-upping the mayor's wife. "Perfect." Then she scowled again, which was easy for her to do because once a face is used to being a certain way, it returns to its original features without any effort at all. "But," she said, "I need it up in the next two hours. You understand, don't you?"

"I do," Charlotte said. "I definitely do."

She walked out the front door of Mrs. McClintock's house and tried not to think about the other fifteen decorations she'd made and hung for the woman—not one of which she'd mentioned. Charlotte ran her hand through her hair. She was slipping; she should've known better than to make two of the same garland for two women in the same social circle, but Charlotte had never been more preoccupied than she'd been the past two weeks.

She climbed into her car and turned the heat to high and dialed Jimmy's number on her cell phone. She leaned back in the seat and waited, but it was his voice mail that picked up. Again.

"Hey, baby. It's me." She paused and stared out the window at Mrs. McClintock's house. "I'm leaving a client's house. She was awful to me. Well . . . anyway. Call me, I guess when you can. I love you." She realized there were tears on her face, and she didn't even know she'd been crying.

She glanced one more time at her phone.

Nothing. Still nothing.

*J*immy had looked down and seen Charlotte's number flash on his cell phone screen, but he had a magazine interview in less than thirty seconds, and if he'd answered her, he'd miss the interview. He'd reasoned that he could call her when the interview was finished.

Milton came from the front of the bus and sat next to Jimmy. "How's it going, man?"

Jimmy stared distractedly at his phone. "Waiting on the *People* phone call. What could they possibly want to ask me?"

"This is for their Christmas issue. Just say what you've been saying all week."

Jimmy looked at Milton. "It's starting to sound like someone else. All these interviews, man. I read them, but the articles aren't about me. I say these things, I know, but then they move the words around and make me sound like someone else."

"You're complaining?"

"No," Jimmy said, running his finger along the mist that had formed on the inside of the window. "I'm just so flipping tired. I just want to . . . sleep."

"Well, you'll be able to do that in the new year."

"The twenty-third," Jimmy said.

"Well, that's why I'm back here to talk to you."

The phone buzzed, and they both looked at it to see the 212 area code for New York City. *"People,"* Milton said. "Answer it. I'll be back when you're done. We're an hour from Raleigh."

𝓛eaving Mrs. McClintock's, Charlotte calculated that Jimmy hadn't answered the phone in two days, and when he called her back it was usually the middle of the night. It wasn't that she didn't want him to have success. God, she just missed him. She put the gearshift into drive and headed in the wrong direction, which she didn't realize until she'd reached the stoplight and had that odd disconnected feeling one has when they've gone the wrong way, or missed an exit, or when someone is missing someone else so badly that the details of life become blurry and unfocused. "Get over yourself," she said out loud.

But that is the thing about the Christmas season: It's difficult to get over hope for more. It is harder than any other time of year to get over "I want." This was and is meant to be the time of year for gratitude and giving, but somehow the spirit gets confused and the "I want" takes over. But by the time Charlotte had reached Kara's house, her mood had changed, and she smiled when her best friend answered the door. Like Mrs. McClintock's face that formed itself into its favorite look, Charlotte's soul moved back into its original delight.

Kara hugged Charlotte. "Hey, what's up?"

"I need to borrow your vintage mercury ornaments for the night. Can I beg?"

"Absolutely. But then you must help me finish sketching out the chapel decorations for the nun in Galway. She needs me to fax them to her by tomorrow."

"Faxing to a nun in Galway. Something about that doesn't sound right."

"I know. Isn't that funny?" Kara laughed, which she'd been doing a lot of lately, what with her wedding now only two weeks away.

Charlotte turned her full attention to her friend and the wedding, remembering the wedding Kara had canceled to reunite with Jack. "The last time you were obsessed with every swatch of fabric, every bouquet, every smallest detail. You're so much more relaxed now."

Kara scrunched up her face. "Yeah, last time I think I was a bit more worried about the wedding than the groom. This time I care much more about the groom than the wedding. I just want to get to Ireland, see where Maeve grew up, and say 'I do' in that sweet chapel."

"Oh, Kara, it's all so amazing." Charlotte sat in the whitewashed ladder-back chair. "Like a miracle. A real one."

"I know." Kara sat next to Charlotte and pulled out a photo of the inside of the chapel. "Okay, so here's the picture. I told the nun I just want white roses on the end of each pew. The chapel is so pure, I don't think I want any other decorations."

Charlotte looked at the photo and ran her pinkie across the edge. "What about some magnolia branches on every other pew? You know, something southern. I can have them sent overnight. We can get them off that tree that you and Jack used to hide in when you were kids."

"Yes," Kara said, jumping up. "Perfect. You're so good at this."

Together the two best friends huddled over the chapel photo and talked about flowers and travel and the Christmas they all waited for.

*M*ilton returned to the bus seat just as Jimmy was dialing Charlotte's number. "How'd the interview go?"

"Same old, same old." Jimmy slammed his phone shut. "Can I have a few minutes alone?"

"Nope, sorry. We'll be in Raleigh in thirty minutes, and I need to talk to you before sound check."

"What is it?" Fatigue pulled at Jimmy's eyes; his insides felt weighed down with concrete, as if he were stuck in his seat.

"Well, look at you. You lost your Christmas cheer?"

"I'm just tired. That's all. I don't think I can hear 'Jingle Bells' one more time."

"Well, you've got—let me count," Milton ticked cities off on his fingers, "—six more times to hear it."

"That doesn't include sound check," Jimmy said, groaning.

"Well, I'm here to cheer you up. I have great news."

"Yes?"

"You have been invited to sing your song at 'The Radio City Christmas Spectacular' on Christmas Eve."

"No can do." Jimmy held up his hand. "I'll be on a plane to Ireland by then."

"You aren't listening to me. You have been invited to sing at Rockefeller Center. Nationally broadcast. Christmas Eve." Milton counted off the reasons on his fingers. "Right now only the country-music fans have heard of your song. That night—on Christmas Eve—the entire world will hear of you. Don't you understand? There are a thousand singers who would kill their mama for this chance. Are you kidding me?"

"Can I think about it?" Jimmy asked.

"Yeah, sure." Milton paused and stared out the window. "For two seconds. That is how long you have to think about it."

Jimmy looked at Milton's face. "You already confirmed, didn't you?"

"Yes."

"Then here is the deal. I'm on a flight to Ireland the minute my song is over. I mean, the *minute*. First class. And you reimburse Mr. Larson for my ticket on the twenty-third. You got it?"

"Look at you, getting a handle on this stardom attitude." Milton smiled. "I think I like it."

Jimmy exhaled. "It's my brother's wedding."

Milton held up his hand. "If anyone would understand why you're doing this, it would be him, wouldn't it? It's for you, but it's also for your brother and for the band. Your band."

"Yeah," Jimmy said and exhaled. "I guess you're right."

Milton walked back toward the front of the bus when Ellie walked back and then sat next to Jimmy. "You okay?"

"I'm good. You?"

"Couldn't be better. I love this Raleigh stadium. You ever sung here?"

Jimmy laughed and shook his head. "I sang in a bar in Raleigh once." He paused. "To six people."

Ellie smiled. "Well, you'd better get used to the bigger places."

"I think I am."

"You getting used to all the attention?"

He shrugged.

"Seriously, you haven't been able to get out of the bus without girls lined up down the street. They wait by the back door of the stadium after the concert. They try to follow us to the bars. Is it making you crazy?"

"It's a little embarrassing," he said.

"I bet you've slept ten minutes every night."

"Well, if y'all would quit dragging me out every night, it might be better." He laughed, but he knew that he could stay back in the bus. But the two nights he'd stayed in, he'd felt the loneliness he didn't want to feel. But he forgot what he already knew—that you can ignore your feelings, but they're there anyway. They stay. And stay. Ignoring them does not make them go away—like a stubborn child.

"Yeah, we're really draggin' you." She laughed. "And we don't have to get up for the 6:00 a.m. interviews. Not that I'd mind."

"Good. Tomorrow morning you can be me." He smiled.

She snuggled back into the chair, curling her legs underneath her. "I don't think they'd believe me."

So," Jimmy said, sticking his phone into his back pocket, "tell me about your family. You haven't told me anything about who you're missing."

"Oh, that's boring." She stared out the window. "Oh, Jimmy, look. It's starting to snow."

Together they stared out the window and talked and laughed until the bus pulled into the stadium in Raleigh, and the whole party started again. And that is what this had all become—a party. What started as one thing became something else. And this is what happens when we aren't careful, when we aren't watching—what starts as one thing becomes something else entirely. Now it was a big party all about Jimmy's fame and adorableness and how many singles of "Undeserved" were downloaded in a day. What began as an expression of love was fast becoming an expression of identity. Jimmy was becoming "the song."

Ellie was correct—there were lines of girls waiting at every stop. The backstage passes went from children and families wanting to meet Rusk and Hope to girls in white tank tops and cowboy boots just dying to meet and touch Jimmy Sullivan.

He stepped off the bus and signed autographs, shook hands, smiled for the cameras. He posed with Santa Claus in a fake sleigh onstage, as if the sleigh were real, as if Santa were real, as if the fame were real. Of course, none of it was, but he did not yet realize it. Not yet.

CHAPTER NINE

Here is where you must be careful:
Not all things are as they appear to be.

—MAEVE MAHONEY TO KARA LARSON

The paperboy rode his bike through the frigid streets of Palmetto Pointe, throwing the plastic-wrapped newspaper over his shoulder with the same move he used for his fastball on the baseball diamond—this is how he practiced and made cash at the same time. He hated this time of year, not only for the cold but also for having to dodge the Christmas decorations people put in their front yards, the strings of lights and wires that caught his bicycle tires in the predawn dark. When he reached Charlotte's house, he threw the paper, not

knowing he was delivering news that should have come another way, that should have come from that ole Jimmy Sullivan himself. If he'd known, if the paperboy had known what
I knew, he would've skipped her house, avoided the neighbor's silly lightbulb red-nosed reindeer, and gone on to the
next driveway. But he couldn't know, and I couldn't stop him.

The announcement in the Palmetto Pointe morning
paper was splashed across the front page: "Palmetto Pointe's
Own Jimmy Sullivan to Sing at Radio City Music Hall on
Christmas Eve."

Charlotte was already standing in the kitchen holding a
cup of coffee and staring out into the beginning of the day
when the thump of the newspaper hit her front porch. She
opened the front door and grabbed the paper. Her mind on
anything but the news, she unwrapped the paper, stuffed the
rubber band in the junk drawer—just like every morning.
The paper flopped open on the countertop, and she read the
headline twice before she understood, before the words held
any meaning. Then her hand shook; coffee splattered across
the counter.

She hadn't spoken to Jimmy in three days, and now she
knew why: He was off in his own land now. He was gone
from her; she'd felt it, and now she knew it.

The article remained unread, the coffee soaking through

the print as Charlotte walked into the living room. Really, why did she need to read the article? The headline told her everything she wanted to know. He'd moved on with this new life. He didn't care enough to tell her he was singing in New York City and he wasn't coming to Ireland. Of course he wasn't. He couldn't be in New York City and Ireland at the same time. She plugged in her prelit, perfectly decorated, but fake Christmas tree. She turned a key for the gas fireplace, threw in a match, and then sat in the threadbare lounge chair, the one she'd been meaning to re-cover but had not yet because she loved the old faded chintz on it now. She exhaled and stared at the tree, at the fake gas fire licking the fake logs, and wished it were all real: the fire, the logs, the tree, Jimmy's love. But they weren't. And maybe none of it ever had been.

*J*immy awoke to his cell phone ringing. He groaned. God, he'd never been so tired. He glanced at the screen, but the leftover whiskey fogged his mind and his eyesight. He answered without knowing who it was.

"Hey, bro! What is going *on?*" Jack's voice bellowed.

"Hey, I'm sleeping. I'm finally getting some shut-eye. Can I call you back?"

"Ah, have you seen the front page of the *Palmetto Pointe Times*?" Jack asked.

Jimmy's irritation rose as it does for all of us when fatigue clouds every emotion into one. "How would I have seen the front page of the *Palmetto Pointe Times* when I'm in Raleigh and I'm asleep?"

Jack's answer was silence, but it really wasn't silence at all. It was an accusatory hissing sound that Jimmy heard in his ear as disapproval.

Jimmy exhaled into the phone. "I'm guessing you want me to ask you what it says, right?"

"Oh, I'm thinking you already know what it says." Jack's voice was low, rough as sandpaper, and Jimmy knew Jack was mad. A brother knows these things.

"Why don't we quit playing this stupid game and you just tell me? If it was important enough to wake me, then just tell me."

"Seems you're singing at Radio City on Christmas Eve. Singing your perfect Christmas song."

Jimmy rubbed his forehead, wished he hadn't had that last shot of whiskey at the bar with Ellie. He groaned. "Damn, I was gonna call you this morning, Jack. I was."

"Okay."

"Milton said yes for me, and how could I possibly turn it down? This could change everything for us. For me. For you. For our band. It's nationally broadcast . . . " Even Jimmy heard Milton's words coming out of his own mouth.

"It's nationally broadcast, and, oh, by the way it's also my wedding."

Jimmy of course knew this, but sometimes the saying of something is worse than the knowing of it, and this was one of those times. "I'm sorry," Jimmy said. "Of all people, you understand, right? I mean this is for both of us. For all of us."

"I don't think so." Jack's voice was quiet now, the anger gone. "Have you talked to Charlotte?"

"I'll call her right now," Jimmy said and sat up. Charlotte. He hadn't told her. His head spun and nausea rose.

"Good idea."

"Jack?"

"What?"

"Man, I'm sorry. Please try to understand. Please. Let me talk to Charlotte, and I'll call you back in a while. I'll meet you in Ireland on Christmas Day night; I'll be there in time for the party, just not the ceremony."

"That's just great, Jimmy. Always in time for the party."

Jack hung up without a good-bye, and Jimmy slumped back into his bunk, felt around for the water bottle, and chugged it before dialing Charlotte's number. It rang what seemed endlessly before her voice mail answered. Jimmy didn't leave a message because he had no idea what to say.

Charlotte heard her cell phone in the kitchen, but she didn't rise.

Kara was there now and sat across from Charlotte, holding her own mug of coffee. "Aren't you going to see if that's him?"

Charlotte shook her head. "No. I won't say anything nice right now, so I think I'll just let it ring."

Kara stared out the window at the morning so bright it looked as though the sun came in through cut glass, sharp and intrusive. "I'm sorry, Charlotte. I don't know what else to say."

Charlotte twisted in her chair. "No, Kara. Do not be sorry. Not you. Listen, I knew what I was getting into loving a singer-songwriter who traveled and lived on a bus. I knew and I chose it anyway. It was sweet . . . Now it's sad. But listen, this will not change your wedding or my excitement for your wedding even one teensy-weensy bit." Charlotte leaned across her chair and looked directly into Kara's eyes. "This is absolutely and completely going to be the most beautiful

Christmas we've ever had. I can't wait to get to Ireland. I can't wait to see Galway."

Kara smiled and reached across the space between them, taking Charlotte's hand. "You are amazing."

Again the phone rang, but this time it was Kara's. She glanced at the screen. "Jimmy," she said.

Charlotte shook her head, and Kara hit "Ignore." Together they sat in silence, sipping their coffee and listening to the morning begin.

Losing a love somehow felt like finding one in this way—falling. She felt as though she were falling, but this time into an emptiness, into an echoing sadness.

CHAPTER TEN

*Whatever is in your life
right now is taking life from you.*
—Maeve Mahoney to Kara Larson

It was December 22 when the plane hovered in the sky with the miracle of flight that Charlotte did not want to spend too long thinking about. She settled back into her seat and flipped through the movie choices. None sounded appealing. It was an all-night flight, and she knew she should sleep; they'd land in Ireland at six in the morning and have a full day ahead, but her thoughts and mind spun around themselves like tangled threads that had become knotted and useless.

Kara and Jack were two rows over, and both appeared to be asleep. Isabelle and Hank were five rows ahead, and she couldn't see them. Porter and Rosie were in first class, and then there was the empty seat next to Charlotte—a visual reminder of an unseen reality that Jimmy was gone from her. She had decided on that morning of the newspaper to focus only on Kara's wedding, on her best friend's joy. She would not think about or talk to Jimmy Sullivan, and she had mostly kept this vow until now, when the missing of him crowded in on her as if a large, obese man sat in the seat next to her, shoving her into the window.

Jimmy had left numerous messages. First he tried explaining, then apologizing, and then the last one was angry. Charlotte had never heard him use that tone of voice before that message, and she'd erased both the message and the memory of the exact words. He'd spoken of her not understanding, of his need to help the band, of his own career.

She now reached into her purse and pulled out the shell that Kara had thrown at her that afternoon Jimmy had announced this tour. She'd believed then—believed in love surviving a music tour, in a fairy tale obviously. Her finger ran across the concave surface worn smooth by the sea, her sadness settling like smoke into the curve of nature's pure white shell.

Outside the plane's window, the sunset spread like ribbons across the line between cloud and universe. Her eyes closed and her thoughts quieted, which is exactly what a sunset can do to a mind—quiet it. She felt a presence next to her body, and she imagined, for that moment between sleep and awake, that moment between knowing and believing, that Jimmy was with her. She opened her eyes to see Kara.

"Did I wake you?" Kara asked.

"No, I think I just was sort of half asleep. For a millisecond I thought you were Jimmy. That he was really here."

"I'm sorry," Kara said. "I looked over at the empty seat, and my heart hurt."

"No. None of that from you," Charlotte said. "This is your wedding. Your time. I am fine."

"You're always fine. I know that, but you're allowed to be sad and fine, doncha think?"

Charlotte ran her finger across the glass window. "Look at that sunset. It lasts longer up here, doesn't it?"

"Huh?" Kara leaned closer to the window.

"The sunset lasts longer up above the clouds. I wonder why. I mean, at home if you turn around or get distracted, you miss the entire beauty, as if it never happened, as if the sun is there and then gone. But not up here. Wow, the sunset has been settling into the clouds for over an hour, lingering there like it's a party it doesn't want to leave."

"You," Kara said, "are adorable."

"I thought it was so beautiful. You know, this sweet attraction that would change everything."

"Are we still talking about the sunset?" Kara asked.

Charlotte turned to her friend. "No." She smiled sadly. "I mean, isn't that what love is supposed to do? Change everything?"

"I guess in a way it did. In a way his love for you did change everything. He wouldn't have written the song . . . if he hadn't loved. He's just lost sight of it. That's all, Charlotte. He's lost sight."

"No, you don't lose sight of love. Love isn't a stickie you just carry around and put on the most convenient place. It *is* or it *isn't.*"

"Of course you can lose sight. Look at Jack and me. I was blind to it until I wasn't."

"That's different."

"Why?"

"Because he didn't choose to leave." Charlotte shrugged. "Jimmy made his choice. He did. There isn't really a way to change that choice."

"As Maeve would have said, 'You must not demand proof to believe.'"

Charlotte turned back to the window, the sun now set, only night dominating the sky obliterating east from west, up from down. "It's gone now."

They both stared into the darkness; the sun on the other side of the earth where unseen forces were at work, forces Charlotte and Kara could *not* and did *not* see. As it should be. The calendar moved from December 22 to December 23 as they slept, and the plane moved across the sky to another land, another day, the minutes ticking backward, as Ireland was six hours ahead. Each minute more than a minute as time and day overlapped.

*J*immy glanced at his watch. It was ten at night on December 22 in Memphis, Tennessee; the band was hanging out for the last night together before everyone went their separate ways. He counted forward—it would be four in the morning for his brother, for Charlotte, in that plane. He should be on that plane, but he would not allow the regret to bounce against his fatigue; he dismissed it, as one would a bothersome child needing attention. He could not be apologetic about making a good choice for himself, and ultimately for his brother and their band.

Ellie sidled up next to him. "Okay, we're gonna go hit Memphis. Blue suede shoes. Elvis. You in?"

Jimmy smiled at Ellie. "No, not tonight. Sleep tonight."

She shrugged and turned to the crew. "He's too good for us now," she said, and her words held no mirth or laughter.

"No," Jimmy said, "that's not it. You know that's not it. You guys are amazing. I just have got to finally lie down."

"You can sleep when you're dead," a crew member called out, throwing a football toward Jimmy.

Jimmy dove for the ball, caught it, and laughed. "Good point. Let's go."

There was something about belonging that always captured Jimmy's heart—belonging to a family or a group or a person at all, really. When someone grows up trying to find their place in a world where there is no place, a soul can sometimes be fooled into believing that it's found a home when really it's merely found a soft area to land that isn't theirs at all. At all.

He grabbed his jacket and followed the group. The tour cities had blurred together, all of them with auditoriums and girls and Christmas carols and Santa hats and lights. He wanted to call Charlotte. It was driving him crazy that she wouldn't speak to him. Why wouldn't she just let him explain? He'd told Jack to please pass on the reasons, to please tell Charlotte that of course he still loved her and this decision had nothing to do with how much he did or didn't love her. But even Jack didn't sound convinced.

The group emerged into the dark, cold night, and Jimmy glanced up at the sky where somewhere far away Charlotte slept in a plane flying toward Ireland. He slipped his hand into his pocket and felt the box that held the ring he'd planned on giving her on Christmas Day. He'd offer it to her the minute he saw her; Christmas was just a day on the calendar, not one more or less than any other day.

This is what he told himself.

Trays up, seats in an upright position, the plane began its descent into Shannon, Ireland, and the earth drew closer, as if a camera lens were pulled in tighter and tighter, slowly revealing the greenest land Charlotte had ever seen. Stone walls spread like creeks and rivers, like snakes through the land, dividing it into puzzle pieces of brilliant green so lush Charlotte thought the color must have a different name, a name larger and more expansive than simply "green." She touched her fingers to the window as if she could draw the lushness into her soul. If there were a land that could heal a heart, it must and could be this piece of earth below the plane.

The runway rose up, or so it seemed, and the plane skidded to a halt. Passengers stretched and gathered their belongings. Charlotte glanced at her watch: 6:10 a.m. Midnight at home.

No, she thought. She would no longer compare there to here. Here, it was a new day. The eve of Christmas Eve.

Kara and Jack waved from their seats, and Charlotte waved back, smiled. Her best friend's wedding. This, she reminded herself, was what to focus on and about. Kara's wedding.

*J*immy sat back in the bar booth, surrounded by the crew, and glanced at his watch. The plane would be landing; they'd all be in Ireland now. He vaguely wondered if anyone had taken his seat, if Charlotte sat with a stranger or alone. It was his last night with the Christmas tour. Tomorrow everyone would go their separate ways, and he alone would fly to New York City for the big event.

Jimmy leaned back and tilted his head. The flashing multicolored Christmas lights were giving him a headache. An itchy, threadbare wreath behind his head scratched his neck. He grabbed at the irritating wreath, threw it onto the bench behind him.

Ellie looked over at the discarded fake greenery and then back at him. "So have your parents ever seen you play or sing?" She shrugged. "I'm just asking. Mine never have. They think it's a waste of time."

Jimmy looked at this wounded young girl. "My mom has a million times. But I don't think my father even knows I sing. Or play. Or am alive."

"I'm sorry," she said.

Jimmy shook his head. "No big deal. It's been a long, long time since I've thought about it."

"Nothing like that is ever a long time ago." She touched his arm. "Don't you want? . . ."

Jimmy held up his hand. "Listen, I don't want anything that in any way has something to do with or about my dad. He's long gone, and good riddance."

Ellie picked up the discarded wreath and hung it back on the hook behind Jimmy's head. "That's why I'm out here on the road during the holidays. So much easier than being home, wherever home is."

Jimmy lifted his glass of whiskey. "Exactly. Wherever home is."

Damn all of it. Jimmy's irritation turned to anger as quickly as a storm turns into a hurricane, building strength, gathering cloud upon cloud, rain upon rain, fury upon fury. Damn his dad and concerts and family expectations. Damn

Charlotte and love and weddings. And seriously, damn Christmas. What a crock, believing that a single day or a single love or a single person could change anything.

When the bar closed, the band and crew walked through the streets of Memphis, bundled up and talking about going home in the morning.

Milton turned to Jimmy. "You, my friend, have a 6:00 a.m. flight to New York."

"I know, I know, I know." Jimmy exhaled. "I'm already packed."

They filed onto the bus, and Jimmy walked back to his bunk, lay down on the hard mattress, and thought of his dad. Jimmy shoved the thought from his mind, yet it returned like thunder in a storm that seemed far off, but was in the backyard. Why, Jimmy wondered, was he thinking about his dad now? He truly didn't care about the old drunk man.

So, if he didn't care about the old man, why was he thinking about him, wondering if he knew about the Unknown Souls or their mother or Jack or anything at all? Through the years he'd often imagined his dad reading about the band or their success, yet Jimmy didn't even know if his dad was alive, much less paying any attention to the whereabouts of his long-gone sons.

He'd imagined his dad reading an article and then calling, saying, "Wow, I'm so proud." Or that Wagner was out in the audience, hiding yet weeping with pride at his boys' talent. But these dreams and imaginings had stopped long ago. Now, if Jimmy did think of it, he hoped his dad experienced regret and sadness. The need, Jimmy thought, for his dad's approval was long gone. Jimmy didn't believe he needed a man he didn't know to be proud of him.

But tonight, with Jack in Ireland, Jimmy felt the old and ancient need to have his dad know and be proud. What Jimmy didn't understand was that there is this need in a man—always present—for a dad's approval. Yet this need is unnecessary because the One that made the man already approves of the man. And, yes, even loves him. Oh, so much loves him.

Jimmy lay back on the cot and closed his eyes. What was he doing this for? This trip to New York City, this distance from the woman he loved, from his brother's wedding?

Approval.

He shook his head against the pillow. No way. It couldn't be. He was doing this for the band, for all of them. Not for his dad. That was ridiculous. He closed his eyes against the stupid thought and fell into the darkest sleep he'd ever had, a sleep that wasn't really a sleep but a deadness that threatened to overtake his heart.

Their baggage came out in sporadic shifts, and the laughing group of Kara, Jack, Charlotte, Porter and Rosie, and Isabelle and Hank counted the bags until they were sure they had everything. Squinting into the morning, they emerged from the airport and into a sun that seemed filtered and washed in green light.

"Ireland," Charlotte said.

Kara lifted her face to the biting wind. "Wow, huh?"

"I thought it was supposed to be all gloomy and dark here in the winter," Charlotte said.

The group raised their eyes to the clearest sky. "It is freezing, though." Jack pulled his scarf tighter. "Okay, let's go find the rental car place. I rented a van for all of us."

After deciphering the signs and tumbling aboard a bus, they emerged at the rental car booth and then followed Jack to the van. When they saw the vehicle, the laughter was simultaneous and free. The van was squat, square, and small enough to fit in the back of Porter's pickup truck at home in South Carolina. There was just no way they were all going to fit into that one car with all the luggage.

"This," Jack said, "is what they call a van? We're going to need another car."

Isabelle sat on her suitcase. "No way I'm driving. I can barely drive down the right side of the road, much less the left side. Plus, I heard these are the skinniest, windiest roads in the world. I'll kill someone."

Jack laughed. "I wouldn't let you drive. But someone is going to have to besides me. This is the largest car they have, and there is no way we're going to fit."

Mr. Larson coughed. "I know it should be me, but I've never driven on the wrong side of the road."

"Dad?" Kara poked at him. "Except that time in Charleston when you went down a one-way street and almost killed all of us."

"Exactly," Mr. Larson said. "But I guess I can try."

"It'll be an adventure," Charlotte said.

"That's what I'm afraid of." Mr. Larson dropped his briefcase and exhaled. "I'll be right back."

The streets wound through the stone-dotted landscape an hour and a half north of the Shannon Airport and into Galway. Charlotte rode with Kara and Jack, her feet crammed underneath the seat to catch the meager heat coming from the floor vents. Together they tried to pronounce every sign they passed: Cappafean and Garheeny More, Ardrahan and Kilcolgan. The ground appeared as if green lumps of earth had pushed their way through dirt and stone, proving their resilience against a ragged landscape like none Charlotte had ever seen. The stones and rocks echoing permanence born in another time, a time so ancient that the person who had set these stones into walls could not have imagined cars or the people in them. A time long gone. Yes, Charlotte thought, it all passes: love, joy, sadness. It is there, and then it is gone, leaving behind only the echo.

She wiped at her eyes, forced her thoughts to happier things. "Pictures didn't catch this," she said from the backseat.

Jack slammed on the brakes. "Hold on!" he hollered, suitcases flying forward, the car skidding sideways. In front of them two stray sheep stood in the middle of the road, staring at them as if the car were the thing that didn't belong, as if the car drove onto their field.

Charlotte burst out laughing. "This is crazy. They just stand in the middle of the road and expect to not get hit."

"Yeah." Kara rolled down her window. "They're looking at us like we're the crazy ones." She waved her hand out the window. "Shoo!" she hollered.

"'Shoo'?" Jack's words were wrapped in laughter. "Did you just yell 'shoo' at the sheep?"

"I did," Kara said and stuck her head back in the window. "You got a better plan?"

Jack pressed his hand on the steering wheel, and a tinny, small noise erupted from the car, a honk that really wasn't a honk at all, but an irritating noise. Charlotte and Kara looked at one another in that way that friends do and then burst into laughter that could not have been stopped by God himself.

Jack stared at them and shook his head. "You think this is funny?"

Kara wiped at tears. "That is the absolute most pitiful honk I have ever heard. My 'shoo' scared them more than that."

A squeal of tire came from behind them, and they all swiveled to see Mr. Larson slam on his brakes and just miss hitting them. Everyone piled out of the cars, laughing.

Kara walked toward the side of the road, waving at the sheep to follow her, which of course they didn't. "Oh . . . ," she said and turned to the group. "Come here." Her voice held reverence as if she'd seen an angel or apparition. And in a way she had.

Then they all saw it; they finally saw it. Galway Bay. The place and view Kara's heart had seen only in imagination, the place she believed brought Jack back to her, the bay where she believed Maeve Mahoney now lived in spirit.

"Oh!" Kara cried out, grabbing Jack's elbow.

Jack glanced to the left, and his breath was also taken away. Only a man with a dead heart would not lose his very breath at this sight. Together the group gathered at the cliff's edge, high above the rocks and waves, floating above the sway of the bay.

The late-morning sunlight scattered across the waves in a shifting pattern of the earth's motion, an intricate ballet. Boats bobbed like toys in the powerful force, and water slammed and scattered against the cliffs, and then gently, impossibly, back into the sea that had just hurled it into the rocks, as if the water was destined to return to the bay only to be flung again. Like love, Charlotte thought. Going back for more to be tossed onto the rocks again.

Kara took Jack's hand. "How is it possible that it is more beautiful than I imagined?"

He didn't answer because he didn't have an answer. He kissed Kara right there overlooking the cliffs. "God, I love you, Kara. I do so love you. If it took a legend from this place to bring you to me, I will love it also."

Kara pushed her face into Jack's sweater and let the tears melt into the wool of his scarf. "I love you."

He leaned down to whisper, so as not to hurt Charlotte's feelings, "I wish Jimmy were here."

She lifted her face and stood on her toes to whisper in his ear, "I know. You didn't have to say it; I know." She kissed the edge of his ear.

Porter looked at his daughter. "Weird how the sheep stopped us right here, right at the first view of the bay."

Kara laughed. "Yeah, you'd think Maeve Mahoney had something to do with it, wouldn't you?"

Isabelle hollered into the wind, "Now, I have to admit this is one of the most beautiful sights I've ever seen, present company included, but I'm freezing my arse off here! Can we see this view from inside a hotel with a warm drink?"

"'Arse'?" Hank asked. "Who says 'arse'?"

Isabelle shrugged and pulled her scarf around her head and face. "When in Ireland, speak as the Irish."

"Okay," Hank said as they all ran back to the cars. "The first Irish guy I meet, I'm asking him if they say 'arse.' Twenty dollars they do not say 'arse.'"

Laughter, holy laughter if I do say so myself, rolled across the bay as they all climbed into their cars and drove up Dublin Street and into Claddagh Village. The village of the myth, the village of Maeve Mahoney, the village where Jack would finally wed Kara Larson.

They stood in front of the Dominican church, staring up at the stone structure as if it were in a movie, or a photograph, something not real.

Kara squeezed Charlotte's hand. "This is it."

Charlotte nodded.

Mr. Larson spoke first. "So this is the church Maeve told you about?"

The frigid wind blew in off the bay behind the crowd, but sometimes the sight in front of your eyes can take your mind off your body. This very church had been here for more than five hundred years. It is a place we call St. Mary on the Hill, a place of the Claddagh Dominicans. Built of Galway granite, this building is, to many, the presence of God in the village, more, oh, how much more, than so many tons of granite and stone. The sacred building stands broad and proud, light gazing out from her tall windows and side doors. Her reflection shines off the water as if there is a church beneath the church, a holy place on which the holy place rests. At the top of the church there is a statue of Mary tucked into a marble enclave, a home of sorts. Mary stares out over the bay and everyone who enters the front door of her church. But there is another Mary, one we call "Our Lady," and she is inside the church.

Kara turned to her friends, to her dad. "This is it. And it's more beautiful, like everything else here, than I imagined. This is where they do the blessing of the bay she told me about. Every year, on a Sunday in mid-August, the entire town comes to the Claddagh pier here for the blessing of the bay and its fishermen. The priest reads and sprinkles holy water. There is this beautiful scene. I can almost see it from the story Maeve told me. The brown sails, the priest, the hymns."

"Can you tell us the story inside?" Isabelle asked. "I'm freezing."

"We're meeting a nun tomorrow afternoon for the rehearsal, but if y'all want to go in now . . . "

Isabelle stood at the double wooden doors, opened them, and swept her hand toward the inside. "Let's go. It's warm in here."

The church doors opened into a foyer, an aisle leading to ornate arched stained-glass windows, where Saint Thomas Aquinas and Saint Dominic looked out over the church with an adoring gaze. Arched columns and ornate mosaics lined the sides of the church, running alongside the pews like children keeping tight to their parents. But it was the wooden baroque statue that caused the group to stop, as if Mary herself had reached out and grabbed them.

"This statue," Kara said as she pointed to a wooden statue of Mary, "was in Maeve's story. I can't believe I'm finally looking at it. In a way I'm stunned it's real. That it's here. It's like waking up and finding part of your dream sitting in your bedroom." Kara laughed, shook her head.

"What part of her story?" Charlotte asked, stepping forward, fascinated by this wooden statue in a way she didn't yet understand.

"Well, she is called Our Lady of Galway. Maeve told me the Spanish priests brought her back from exile, along with the first rosaries. She was cleaned in Dublin and brought back here with this huge parade and celebration. Maeve was in the procession that brought the statue to the church; she was with the boy she loved—Richard, who her story was all about. It was the next morning that he was taken from the village. Maeve said she prayed to *this* Mary to bring him back safely. I feel a bit like Alice in Wonderland wondering what's real and what's not."

"Hey," Jack said, "I'm real. Back to me, okay?" His voice held that sweet laughter Kara had loved since memory began.

She looked at him. "Sometimes I'm not even sure that's true or real."

Mr. Larson coughed. "Well, if none of this is real, then I don't have to pay for it, right?"

Kara smiled and then pointed to the glittering mosaic behind the statue. "That is the blessing of the bay. She watches over that also."

The group walked away and toward the sacristy, but Charlotte stood to stare at the Mary statue, at Our Lady of Galway, an ornately carved wooden statue of Mary holding her son, cradling baby Jesus in the crook of her left arm. Set into the wooden base were three carved angels' faces peaking out from under Mary's dress, which billowed as if a strong wind blew in off the bay. Her eyes stared out, yet seemed to slightly glance down toward the left, toward her son, but also toward the world, toward Charlotte. Baby Jesus's face was placid and somehow simultaneously ancient and innocent; he held out his right hand as if waving or blessing or maybe even stopping someone from coming near. Charlotte would like to believe he was blessing anyone or anything that passed. A long mother-of-pearl rosary hung from Mary's fingers, which were curled in a gesture so delicate, it was as if she held the most fragile thing in the world. From the bottom of the rosary chain, an ornate cross dropped like a tear in front of the angels' faces.

Charlotte stepped back. "So, what do you think about what we've all done about your son's birthday? I bet you have a thing or two to say about it, don't you?"

Mary, of course, didn't answer but gazed out, holding tight to her son as if to say, "I only care about him. I love him."

Charlotte imagined and, yes, almost heard those words, so much so that she answered. "Yep, I know how that feels— to love. Not like that, maybe, but love, yes." She glanced behind her to make sure no one else heard her, and then she whispered to Mary, "I know you're busy being a mom and all, and that this is a crazy time of year for you, but if you have any influence over things, could you bring Jimmy to his senses? Let him know that this birthday, this birthday of your son's, is about so much more than fame and parties. Please let him know it's about love. And just that. Just love."

Charlotte reached into her purse and set the small gray-white shell, which Kara had given her that day at the beach when Jimmy had told them all about the Christmas tour, at the base of the statue, right next to the angels' placid faces.

Mary appeared as if she didn't care, but you never know who's listening, do you?

CHAPTER ELEVEN

You must not demand proof to believe.
—Maeve Mahoney to Kara Larson

The Irish pub was warm, the lights dim, and the group of travelers struggled to keep their eyes open. Their rooms weren't ready yet, and they'd all agreed to stay awake until at least dark when they could sleep and start fresh in the morning, but they were fading quickly.

"Okay," Kara said. "Let's finish talking about plans. That way we'll all stay awake."

"Yeah, that always makes me stay wide awake," Jack said. "Logistics."

She pushed at him so he fell off the bench of the pub booth and landed on the floor, sprawled and laughing. "I think I just landed on my arse."

The waitress came toward them and looked down at Jack on the floor. "Okay, should we cut him off this early in the evening?" Her Irish accent added a note to each syllable.

Jack jumped up and shook his head at the waitress. "Don't pay any attention to them. They've been flying all night, and they thought pushing me to the floor on my arse was a funny joke."

"Arse?" she asked.

Hank leaned across the scarred bar table. "You can settle a bet here once and for all. Do the Irish say 'arse'?"

The waitress smiled at them, glancing from one to the next. "Okay, where are you from?"

"Palmetto Pointe, South Carolina," Kara answered, scooting over to allow Jack back onto the bench, kissing his cheek and mouthing, "Sorry."

He pinched the end of her nose and then glanced back at the waitress. "A wedding."

"Ah, so I've heard," she said. "You must be the group from the States getting married on Christmas Day in the church here."

"That we are," Kara said.

"How grand. From what I hear, old Maeve Mahoney had something to do with this?"

"That she did," Jack said, attempting to imitate her Irish accent and sounding a bit more like he was trying to imitate a Jamaican accent.

"Oh!" Harry hollered across the table. "I wouldn't be trying that accent again, my man."

The waitress shook her head. "Okay, I'm Moira. Tell me what you need."

"Sleep," Charlotte called out.

"Well, you won't be getting any of that in here, what with the Shenanigans going on soon."

"The what?"

"That's the name of the band coming in any minute. If you can sleep through them, you can sleep through anything."

While they waited on their food and drinks, Kara rattled off the last-minute plans. "So, we'll have a quick rehearsal before the Christmas Eve mass at the priory, and then we'll have a dinner at the hotel restaurant. Then the bride will get her beauty sleep, and we'll meet at the church by ten Christmas morning." She glanced at Charlotte. "Do you think those magnolia leaves showed up?"

"What leaves?" Jack asked.

Kara smiled at him. "It's a surprise. I'll explain later."

He shook his head. "You girls are crazy. Leaves. Whatever."

After a round of drinks and fish and chips, the band did indeed come in, set up their fiddles and guitars, and begin to play Irish music that filled the room and the hearts of everyone at the table.

"Wow!" Kara hollered across to Charlotte. "Jimmy would love these guys!"

Charlotte gave a sad smile. "Yeah, I bet he would."

Kara slapped her hand over her mouth. "I'm such an idiot. I am such a moron. That is what no sleep does to me. I'm sorry, Charlotte."

Charlotte shook her head. "No, you're right. He'd love them."

Jack reached across the table, squeezed Charlotte's hand, but didn't say a word. The dancing had started up full force by now, and words were buried beneath the stomps, laughter, the fiddle and pan flute. A man from the crowd reached down and grabbed Charlotte, pulling her into the pressing and dancing throng.

Charlotte was dizzy with the Guinness, the sleepless plane ride, and the loud music; she protested but to no avail. The man with the dark beard, the blue eyes, and the cragged face of a fisherman took her onto the dance floor and twirled her in circles, laughing. Kara and Jack joined Charlotte and the unknown man.

Isabelle watched this scene from the bench, and tears filled her eyes. Jimmy, damn him, should be here for his brother, for this magical and mystical moment where they danced at the edge of a bay in another land. She grabbed Jack's cell phone, took a quick picture, and e-mailed it to Jimmy. Then she erased the photo and snuck Jack's phone back into his coat pocket.

Hank leaned over. "What did you just do?"

"Showed that ole Jimmy Sullivan that he's a fool. A big, grand fool."

"Isabelle . . . " His voice trailed off like a father reprimanding a child.

She held up her hand. "You be minding your own business now."

He laughed. "You, my dear, can't do an Irish accent any better than Jack. Now get up and dance with me."

And they did, and then last but most important, so did Porter and Rosie. They all danced to the lyrics and melody of an ancient time, an old Claddagh song sung in Gaelic, words they understood only in their hearts.

∞

The streets of New York City were packed, pushing Jimmy Sullivan as if he were invisible. And this is how he felt: invisible. The noon sun beat down, and yet it held no warmth, the air frigid and still, like he had somehow been stuck inside a refrigerator. Or freezer.

He glanced at his cell phone, and although he knew it futile, he hoped that Charlotte had called from Ireland. If she hadn't returned his calls when she was in South Carolina, why would she call from another country on another sea? And yet and always hope has its own heartbeat, and hope still hopes even when we tell it not to care.

Jimmy then scrolled through his e-mails and saw there was one from Jack, but he didn't open it. The crowd pushing him toward Rockefeller Center, he allowed himself to be carried along like flotsam on the incoming tide and then stood in front of the famous Christmas tree. He knew that the tree was huge, but photos, postcards, and TV didn't do it justice, as its size was beyond his expectations. Thousands of lights flickered in the thick and widespread branches. Bulbs the size of his head were bobbing in the wind. A fence surrounded the tree, and Jimmy stood staring up and down, unable to see the entire tree at once. A commotion of voices and laughter bubbled up to the right, and Jimmy turned. A bearded man held his hands up in the air and hollered, "She said yes!"

Laughter and clapping joined the evening, and even Jimmy found himself smiling. This total stranger had just proposed to another total stranger, and yet the anonymous crowd joined in the joy as if they all needed a reason to celebrate, as if this couple's elation could also fill their hearts. Jimmy's chest ached with loneliness, and he stepped back from the fence, turned away from the celebration. He'd just go to bed, just sleep until his performance tomorrow, and then go straight to those he loved. He could make it another two days. Yes, he could. He gritted his teeth.

The hotel was warm and inviting, the bundled-up doorman opening the glass doors and welcoming Jimmy into the foyer where a fireplace and Christmas tree cuddled up next to a menorah.

He checked into his room, and then threw his backpack onto the floor. After ordering pizza and a shot of whiskey from room service, he stared out the window and watched the crowd below, thought how everyone had their own pain, their own demons, their own sleepless nights and haunted choices. He thought of how he'd probably lost Charlotte with his own choices, yet still his emotions swung from anger to loss to hope.

He sat on the bed and took the pad off the faux-mahogany desk and wrote the first lyrics that came to him:

I can't tell my heart what to do.
I can't demand it stop hoping for you.

He wrote until his eyes wouldn't stay open, and then he checked his cell phone one more time—hoping, yes, still hoping—and then closed his eyes.

*C*harlotte and Kara stood at the threshold of the door to their Claddagh hotel room, and their laughter started at the exact same moment.

"Are you kidding me?" Kara asked. "That's a bed?"

"They look like those bunks we stayed in when we went to the awful camp in North Carolina in high school." Charlotte entered the room, threw her purse onto a chair. "But look at that view."

Kara walked to the window, and together they stared out at the bay and the long-necked swans dancing on the water as if they were at a formal affair in their finery.

"Wow," Kara said. "And I'm so tired I bet I could sleep on the floor at this point anyway."

"What a great day and night," Charlotte said. "I love when there's a wide-open day like that and you don't know what could possibly happen, and then only the best things in the world happen and not one of them was planned."

Kara shook her head. "Now, I love you for a million reasons, but here right now is one of them. I know you're sad. I know you miss Jimmy. I know he broke your heart, but here you are looking at our day through the lens of joy."

"I am sad, but this day was like a little miracle in the middle of ordinariness." Charlotte ran her finger down the windowpane. "You know?"

"Yes, I do," Kara answered.

They each fell back onto the bed, and Kara mumbled, "I don't think I can even get up to brush my teeth." But Charlotte didn't answer because she was already asleep, her breathing even and quiet on top of the down comforter where she lay fully dressed.

Jimmy Sullivan's hotel room phone rang its jangly, broken sound. Confused and disoriented about his whereabouts and the time, city, or day, Jimmy fumbled for the earpiece until his hand landed on the cold case and he lifted it to his ear. "What?"

"Mr. Sullivan?"

"Yes," Jimmy answered, clearing his throat in case this was again the press.

"Your father is down here, and he says he needs to see you. May I give him your room number?"

"I think you've got the wrong room. I don't have a father."

"I'm sorry to bother you, Mr. Sullivan."

The operator hung up, and Jimmy rolled back into the pillow. Damn. He'd been sound asleep, a place he'd longed to be for a month now. The phone rang again, and he groaned.

"Hello," he said, glancing now finally at the clock: 11:00 a.m. In a quick calculation he estimated it was 5:00 in the evening in Ireland—Christmas Eve.

"Sir, this is the front desk again, and I'm sorry to bother you, but this man has shown his ID and is insistent that he is related to you and needs to see you."

"Can you put him on the phone?"

There were fumbling noises, and then Jimmy heard the gruff, gravelly voice he would have known after a million years or more. His father. "Jimmy, son, it's me." There was a long pause as this man's voice traveled from childhood to adulthood. Then he spoke again. "Your dad. It's me."

Jimmy's instinct was to hang up, but his hand shook and he sat up in bed. "What?"

"Listen, I know this is crazy. But I'm downstairs in the lobby. Can you come down and see me?"

"No," Jimmy said and stared around the room. Where was he? New York. Yes, New York.

"Son, I've been waiting for you for ages. Just give me five minutes."

Jimmy's heart raced in that thick-thumping way that makes a chest feel as if it has been filled with air too quickly. He rubbed his forehead, stood, and opened the curtains to the room, allowing the late and glaring morning sun into the room. The sunlight flashed off high-rise windows, lit window answering lit window in some secret language. "Five minutes. That's it."

"Got it. Thanks, son," the voice from the past said in quiet gratitude.

Son. When was the last time he had been called son by his father? Jimmy rubbed his head on the way to the shower. His head hurt; his body hurt; his heart raced. What was going on? He stepped into the hot water and allowed it to awaken him. Then without shaving, he threw on his jeans, boots, and a black sweater. With a last quick glance at his weary face, he opened the door to his hotel room and exhaled to go face his father. His father.

The elevator doors opened, and Jimmy stared out into the lobby, trying to find his father before his father saw him. He wanted, in some small, victorious way, to be the first to recognize the other. The man stood thin and alone, leaning against the wall next to the fireplace, as if the wall held him up. Wagner Sullivan stared toward the other bank of elevators, his face furrowed and tight, chewing his bottom lip while he rubbed his hands together. He wasn't the large man Jimmy remembered, as if time, memory, or liquor had shrunk him, or maybe it was some vital combination of all three that diminished this man he'd once called dad.

Jimmy stepped forward and stared at this man for a moment before he decided how to call his name. "Wagner," Jimmy said out loud.

Wagner turned now and stared at Jimmy, his eyes filled with tears; Jimmy looked away from the pain. He would not be suckered into thinking this man had a heart or cared about anything other than his drink, his next drink. Jimmy took three steps forward and held out his hand to shake. Wagner looked down at Jimmy's hand and then smiled a sad smile. "No hug for the old man?"

Jimmy dropped his hand and shook his head. "You aren't my old man."

Wagner nodded. "Okay, fair enough. I figured you hated me, but hoped . . . "

"Well, don't hope anymore." Jimmy heard the callousness in his own voice, but he couldn't stop the hate from emerging. It was an ancient revulsion he'd thought long gone, but it rose from the place of childhood, a distant land that really wasn't so far away at all.

Wagner cringed. "Can we sit down?" He motioned to a couch on their right.

Jimmy sat on the far end of the couch. "Okay, what are you doing here?"

"Well," Wagner sat and faced his son, "I had this entire speech planned. But now I've forgotten the way it went."

Now Jimmy smelled the familiar aroma: whiskey. He felt the nausea of fear rise in his belly. This sweet-sour aroma had meant only and always fighting, yelling, slammed doors. "You're drunk," Jimmy said.

"No." Wagner shook his head. "Maybe this would be easier if I were. Listen, Jimmy. I know you must hate me. I know that. But just let me say a few things, okay?"

Jimmy nodded. "As long as you know I don't have anything to say to you."

"I know that."

Wagner took in a long breath and leaned back onto the couch cushions. "I have one chance to say this, so I'll do my best. I love you, Jimmy. I love Jack. I always have."

"Yep. Beating us was a great way to show that."

"I am here to say sorry. To apologize. The liquor ate me alive. It ate us alive. It killed me inside, and when that inside part was dead I did things that I, as a man, would never have done. I don't know where it happened or how it happened, but one day I was a man with a family and a wife and two brilliant sons, and the next I was facedown in the street while your mother drove all of you into the dawn light and out of my life. It's not that I blame the liquor; I just blame myself for becoming the liquor." Wagner looked away.

Jimmy nodded because an unbidden lump rising in the back of his throat would now allow words.

"I live here in the city. I have for ten years now. When your mama took y'all away, I hit the road. I wandered for years. I tried to find you, but your mama did a good job of making sure I couldn't. I still don't know where you've been all these years. I came here and somehow found myself in a rehab facility that was more like a dungeon, but I did get clean." He turned away. "I'm the janitor for a church on Fiftieth Street. I live in an apartment at the bottom of the church. It's not much of a life, but it's a life. At least it's that." Wagner paused, and stared toward the front door.

Jimmy found his voice. "How did you find me?"

"I've followed your career for years. When I saw you were coming to New York, I made a few phone calls until I found the concert organizer. He told me where you were staying."

"Damn Milton." Jimmy shook his head.

"You look great, son. Please, although I know I don't have the right, please tell me how you're doing. Tell me about Jack. Please." Wagner's face shook as he fought the tears that already sat in the corners of his eyes.

Jimmy stared at this man, at his father, and sorrow rose up next to the anger and whispered, *Have mercy.*

Jimmy summarized the places they'd lived and then continued, "Well, Mama is in California. If you've been following the band, then you know what we've been up to. We're fine. Doing fine. Jack is in Ireland right now. He's getting married tomorrow. I'm here for the performance, and then I'm flying to Ireland. We've been living off the bus for a while now, but Jack and Kara will live in Palmetto Pointe."

"He went back to Palmetto Pointe to find her?"

"Well, actually, Kara found him."

"He's marrying the girl next door. Wow."

Jimmy nodded. Wagner settled further back into the couch.

Silence fell between them until Wagner stood. "Well, I promised I'd only bother you for five minutes, and it's been more than that. I don't want to break another promise to you. I just needed to see your face, to tell you I never stopped loving you, and that I'm sorrier than any man could be. I've never been able to find my way. But you and Jack have always been on my mind. Always. Every day. Please tell Jack." Now the man did begin to cry, large tears rolling down his wrinkled cheeks as he looked down at Jimmy. "I can't buy a ticket to hear you tonight, but I'll be outside in case I can hear something . . . "

Jimmy stood to face the man. "Why did you come here, Wagner?"

"I just told you." He didn't reach to wipe away a single tear, allowing them to settle as puddles in the wrinkles of his face.

"No, really. Why? The real reason. Do you want forgiveness? Did you expect me to invite you to the concert? Did you want to see Jack?"

Wagner shook his head. "No. I came to tell you I'm proud of you. I came because I love you. I'm not the man I ever wanted to be, but that doesn't change the way I feel about you or your brother. That is why I came. That's all." Wagner looked, for the first time in twenty years, directly into his son's eyes and then turned and walked away.

Jimmy watched as his father pushed open the double doors and then glanced back with a smile. A sad smile. Wagner then disappeared into the outside crowd, and Jimmy stood in the lobby for a full five minutes before he began to shake with emotions he couldn't name. The whiskey aroma remained, and Jimmy realized, in that moment of gut-plummeting recognition, that it was not his father he'd smelled, but his own breath. The aroma was from his own sweat and his own life, as if there were a mirror or shimmer of apparition showing Jimmy who he was becoming. Not yet who he was, but who he could be.

Jimmy returned, trembling, to his hotel room, as if he'd just left an odd dream. He ordered breakfast from room service and then sat at the desk, staring at the song about hope that he'd written last night. Hoping. Yes, he'd always hoped his father knew about him, was proud of him. But if that was all he ever wanted, why did he still feel empty and hollowed out? Why did he feel as if he'd been punched in the chest?

He ate his breakfast in silence and then decided that a long, cold walk would clear his head. He threw on his coat, and by the time he stood on the corner of Fifth Avenue and Fifty-second Street, he was overcome with the need to talk to Jack. He pulled out his phone and called. But of course there was no answer. It was 6:00 p.m. in Ireland, and they would all be at the rehearsal or the dinner celebration where Jimmy was supposed to be the best man, supposed to be making a toast.

Jimmy finally looked at the e-mail Jack had sent the night before; he opened the photo and stood in the freezing cold, shivering, waiting for the picture to load. Then he stared at Jack, Kara, Charlotte, and a dark-haired Irish man dancing in front of a band. Charlotte's head was back, and he knew her look of laughter.

Regret snuck up behind him, pushed him, and grabbed him around the middle where his ribs contracted; he released a groan. My God, what was he doing here? If proving himself were the point, then the man who just came to his hotel would have been enough. Would anything ever be enough? As he'd written in his song, only Love was enough. Only that.

He stared again at the phone. He was missing his brother's wedding. He had broken Charlotte's heart. All in the name of what?

Not love. Not that.

His mind began to toss through the options: He could leave for Ireland right now and get there on time, but he didn't have a credit card or enough cash to buy a ticket. He flicked open his phone and called the airlines to find the next flight.

The airline employee's voice was flat and lifeless, as if it were a recording or a piece of cardboard with a voice. "Yes, there is only one flight today, and it leaves in about two hours."

"How much would it be to change my ticket from tomorrow to today?"

The employee continued with all the vital information in the most unvital voice. He had an hour and a half to make an international flight and pay for a ticket when he had no money, no credit card. Impossible.

He groaned. "Can't I just transfer my ticket? I don't have that . . . " He stopped.

The crowd pushed him toward the wall where a woman who looked to be homeless was wearing a thick white down jacket that covered her from neck to feet. Over the jacket were pinned frayed, dirty angel wings. She smiled at Jimmy, and he looked away, not wanting to be asked for a handout. He was down to his last cash until he got paid his full promise next week. A drunken man jostled into Jimmy, shoving him into the angel. "Sorry," he mumbled to her, slamming shut his phone.

"It's no problem, son. But you look miserable. You okay?"

He stared at this old, tattered woman, whose voice did not match her cragged face and dirty clothes. "Yeah, I'm fine."

She smiled. "You looking for a pawnshop?" she asked.

"No," he answered, beginning to run back toward the hotel for his backpack. His luggage had not yet arrived from the tour. All he had on him was Charlotte's ring and his wallet with very little cash. Then he stopped and turned, staring at the angel. "Yes, I am. I am."

"Right there," she said, pointing down the block. "Four doors down on the right."

Jimmy stared at the woman; she'd just answered his question without knowing she had. She'd led him without even knowing he needed to be led. That was how he'd get the money: Charlotte's ring. He could come back after Ireland and buy her ring back, but all that mattered now was getting on that flight that left in an hour and a half.

He ran toward the pawnshop.

It was Christmas Eve day, and the group, which now included Deidre and Bill and Brian, who had landed only hours ago, stood in front of the church, waiting for the director to meet them for the rehearsal. They'd all scattered during the day, some touring Galway, others resting and reading. Charlotte and Kara had wandered the streets, alleyways, and museums of Galway, where Kara took photos of Christmas lights for her new portfolio. They attempted to find the places Maeve had spoken about, walk the path she had walked, take photos of her land and time. They visited the jewelry store, which purported to make the original Claddagh ring, the ring of legend. Kara had asked to meet the owner, but was told she was out of town and would return in the morning.

Deidre yawned and then shivered in her down jacket. "This is beautiful, Kara. Simply amazing."

Charlotte entered the church first, and the others followed. She winked at the Mary statue, glancing down to see the shell still resting as an offering.

The wedding party went through the wedding motions with the church coordinator, Iona. When they stood at the altar, each in their place, the coordinator, in her soft Irish accent, asked Kara, "Would you like me to place the leaves tonight? I think our congregation would love to see them, to know they came from where Maeve lived the last of her life."

"What leaves?" Jack asked.

Kara smiled. "I have a surprise for you." Then she looked to Iona. "If you'll tell me where they are, I'll get them."

Iona held up her hand. "They are back in the sacristy. They came last night. I haven't unpacked them."

Kara followed Iona, and when she returned she held a single magnolia leaf in her hand. She walked toward Jack, who leaned against a pew. "This," she said with this sweet smile on her face, "is from the tree where we used to hide when we were kids. I sent enough to put on each pew's end."

Jack, who had held it together quite nicely until this moment, fought the tears rising in his throat and eyes. "Kara," he said in a tender, quiet voice. "My God, I am the luckiest man in the world. I just am."

She kissed him right there in that church in front of family, friends, and Iona, in front of God and Our Lady of Galway and Saint Thomas Aquinas, and the angels rejoiced. They did. Trust me. They always do when love presides.

*J*immy Sullivan had sold the ring for half of what he'd bought it for, but it was enough cash to get a ticket to Ireland if and only if he got to the airport in time. He ran to hail a cab. The Christmas Eve crowd pushed into stores, hotels, and high-rises. He stood at the curb and exhaled when he felt wetness fall onto his hand, a teardrop, or what looked like a teardrop, landing on his cell phone screen. He glanced up. Snow. Falling from an invisible source, the flakes were large, oversized, and melting on impact. Tumbling onto and over one another, the whiteness filling the sky and gathering its strength.

"No," he mumbled and shoved his phone into his pocket. He noticed another cab approaching and flagged it down, and when it stopped he moved toward the back door. A woman in all black jumped out of the backseat, and the cabbie yelled toward Jimmy, "Off duty!"

Jimmy leaned down toward the window. "I'm desperate. I need to get to the airport for a plane that leaves in less than two hours."

The cabbie didn't even answer, but drove away, leaving Jimmy jumping back onto the curb, where he bumped into a young child dressed as a star. Her face was surrounded by bright-yellow plastic or maybe it was foam. Either way her head had been transformed into a huge star. "Sorry," he said.

"That's okay," the little girl said. "We're late too."

A woman, probably her mother, bundled up in a black fur coat, glared at Jimmy. "Excuse me," she said and grabbed the little girl's hand, pulling her toward a long black limousine.

"Wait, Mother," she said and walked toward Jimmy. "Will you miss your plane?"

Jimmy nodded; she must have heard him begging the cabbie. "If I don't get a cab I will."

"Where are you going?"

Jimmy smiled at her star face. "Ireland."

"Wow," she said. "That far, far away?"

"Yes," he said, enchanted with the flecks of light and dark playing in her eyes. Snow fell harder now, landing on her eyelashes and black parka. "That far away."

"You want to spend Christmas with someone you love." Her voice was clear, like the bells of a church ringing midnight. And he realized she wasn't asking a question, she was telling him the truth.

He smiled at her. "Where are you going all dressed up like a star?"

"I'm the guiding star in the Christmas Eve pageant tonight. I really don't do anything but stand there, but I guess I'm still important. The shepherds won't get there without me."

He smiled and almost patted her on the head but thought better of it with her mother staring at them. "Go be a star. Your mama's waiting."

"You won't get there without me, either," the little girl said in a quiet voice.

"Pardon?" Jimmy asked.

"Mother," the girl said and turned to the woman, "this man has to get to the airport right now or he will spend Christmas all alone."

"Dear, I'm quite sure that man knows how to get a cab."

The little girl stared at her mother for so long that Jimmy began to walk away.

"Come back," the little girl said.

Jimmy stopped, turned.

"No," the woman in the black coat said, "we can't, Maria. We can't save the entire world. You've got to stop this."

"It's not the whole world. It's one man. Imagine, Mother, if you were alone tonight and stuck somewhere. Roger will just be sitting there waiting for us. Why can't he take this sad man to the airport?"

The woman looked at Jimmy, and her face held so many conflicting emotions Jimmy couldn't decide whether she was mad, sad, or irritated with her young daughter. Then she took in a deep breath. "I'm sorry," she said to Jimmy. "I don't mean to be rude at all. The holidays, God, they kill me. I don't think this is the way it's supposed to be. If you can spare another five minutes, our driver will drop us off at church, and then I'll tell him to take you to the airport while Maria is in her play. She's right. He'll have time."

"Ma'am," Jimmy said, "that is too generous. I can't accept."

"Yes, you can. Consider it a Christmas present. Now, don't stand here and talk me out of it. We're late and so are you."

"Thank you," Jimmy said, "You have no idea . . . " And then his voice broke as he crawled into the backseat of the limousine as the woman explained the situation.

Roger, the driver, looked back to Jimmy. "I recognize you, man. You're that country singer that was on TV last week. You seriously want to make an international flight that leaves in less than two hours?"

"Yes," Jimmy said.

"That'll take a miracle, but I'll do my best."

A miracle, yes, but there are such things. Oh, yes, there are.

CHAPTER TWELVE

What fills the eyes fills the heart.
—Old Irish proverb

The lights strung around the room twinkled like stars hung for Kara and Jack, for this moment. Although Charlotte knew they'd been hung for Christmas, tonight it felt as if everything was there for love's final promise. The restaurant was full with families and patrons while the small Larson-Sullivan wedding party gathered at one long table in the back of the restaurant.

Charlotte stood and lifted her champagne glass. "Okay, as the maid of honor, I get to make the toast."

Everyone raised their Waterford flutes, and Charlotte looked over at Kara and Jack. "Here's to Maeve Mahoney and her story, to the story that brought you together."

"Hear! Hear!" echoed across the table.

"And to Kara for recognizing the truth inside the story," Charlotte said and blew a kiss down the table.

This was the place and space where the best man would make his toast—that kind of silence echoed. Finally, Brian stood. "My turn." He looked to Charlotte and smiled and then turned to his sister and Jack. "I would not and could not have picked a better brother if I'd tried. Welcome to the family."

Brian said more, but Charlotte stared out into the dark night and could not stop her mind from wandering to Jimmy. This was the part where he'd read that speech he'd worked on for weeks. This was the part where he'd sit next to Charlotte and hold her hand and whisper that he loved her. This was the part . . .

Charlotte stopped her thoughts from going any further because in truth this was the part where she missed him and her heart broke for all that could have been and was not. She turned her eyes and concentration back to Jack and Kara, lifted her champagne, and took a long swallow.

Brian leaned close to her. "You okay?"

Charlotte nodded. "I'm sad for Jack, too. His brother should be here for him. I want to be mad at Jimmy, but I can't." Quick tears flashed in her eyes. "I keep trying to be mad at him, but I . . . can't."

"Crazy thing this love thing is," Brian said and shook his head. "I'm trying to stay away from it." He lifted his champagne and clinked his glass with hers.

Charlotte smiled at him. "Good luck with that."

The snow in New York City fell in clumps, hitting the limousine windshield and melting on impact. Jimmy glanced at his cell, saw the battery level was low, and dialed Milton's number. His stomach dropped in dread; he knew this was not going to go well.

"Hey, man," Milton answered. "Your luggage is only an hour away from the hotel. This snow is screwing everything up. I'm sorry. Your guitar and clothes will be there in time for the performance. No worries."

Jimmy exhaled, closed his eyes. "I'm not worried, Milton, because I'm not there. I'm on my way to the airport. I should have never agreed to miss my brother's wedding."

"Please tell me you're kidding. Please tell me you're sitting in the hotel room fuming because you need your luggage and guitar. Please."

"Sorry." Jimmy cringed at the word.

"Turn around now. There is no way I am telling Radio City to take you off the schedule. No way. This is my reputation, James Sullivan."

"And this is my family, Milton. The only family I have."

Milton's response can't be repeated here, but I'll just tell you that Jimmy ended up hanging up the phone and leaning his head against the window. The traffic on the Belt Parkway crawled at less than ten miles per hour, and Jimmy leaned forward to Roger. "We gonna make it?"

"I don't think so. I'm sorry. I'm trying."

Jimmy leaned back in the seat. Time took on another dimension, one in which every minute meant a change in his destiny, in all that was important to Jimmy Sullivan, and there he sat without any control over the situation.

Slowly they inched toward JFK, until they arrived with just under an hour until takeoff. Jimmy thanked Roger and took his card so he could send him some money later. Roger smiled. "It was my pleasure. Better than sitting and waiting. I hope you make it."

"Me too." Jimmy ran toward the doors and to the airline counter. He stopped short when he entered the lobby. A line snaked through the makeshift lanes—hundreds of people. He quickly scanned the crowd and found an airline employee.

"Excuse me." Jimmy stopped the employee, noticed the

name Joe on his name tag. "Excuse me, Joe, but I'm trying to make a flight that leaves in less than an hour, and the line looks at least twice that."

Joe laughed. "Ain't no way, buddy. Sorry."

"Listen," Jimmy said, "this is sort of an emergency."

"It always is." Joe began to walk away.

Jimmy closed his eyes to regain his composure, and his heart sent forth the most fervent wish, the most desperate hope to see Charlotte, to see Jack, to be in Ireland before the wedding. Then he ran after Joe. "Please. I am supposed to be in Ireland for my brother's wedding and . . . "

Joe looked at Jimmy and shook his head. "International travel requires you to be here at least two hours before departure."

"I know. I know. But I also know that the flight I need to be on is sitting at the gate and I don't have any luggage. Not even a carry-on. It's Christmas Eve. Come on, can you help me out? What would you do if you were in my situation, needing to see your family?"

Joe stood still for a moment, looking over Jimmy's head and then back at him. "I'd give anything to be with my family tonight. Guess I could at least help you do that."

Jimmy's smile could not have been more authentic.

"Come with me. I'm not sure we can do this, but we'll try."

"Thanks. Serious unbelievable thanks." Jimmy followed the man to a counter.

"No promises." Joe clicked on a computer, began to punch in numbers. "Your ticket?" He held his hand out.

Jimmy cringed. "Well, see, there's a problem there too. I have a ticket for tomorrow, and I know there's a huge change fee. But I have the cash."

Joe looked up at him, shaking his head. "You just trying to make this as difficult as possible?" But he had a smile on his face, and Jimmy handed him the ticket and then the cash for the change fee. While Joe worked on the ticket, Jimmy counted his money. He had enough left to maybe get a rental car. He'd figure that part out when he got there.

After what seemed like an eternity of button punching, Joe looked up with this grin of satisfaction. "You just aren't going to believe this. There is one more seat, and the plane is delayed due to weather. Deicing takes time. Planes are backed up." Joe handed a ticket to Jimmy. "Crazy."

The relief that spread through Jimmy made him dizzy. "Merry Christmas, Joe. I wish you the most merry Christmas you've ever had. Ever."

"You too." Joe's smile proved, once again, that giving offers as much or more to the giver as the receiver. Always.

∽

Waiting at the gate, Jimmy dialed Jack's number, calculating that they were all in the middle of the rehearsal dinner. No one answered, and Jimmy settled back into the plastic seat, staring at the screen for updates on flight departure. He decided not to leave a message. What if the plane didn't leave on time or at all? He held on to his ticket and wished for a hot shower, his luggage, and a shave. He'd roll into Ireland looking like a disheveled vagabond. But then again, better to show up as he was and always has been than not to show up at all.

He turned off his phone to preserve what little battery life it had left. He grabbed a piece of pizza. Time crept on as Jimmy thought of the events of the past several hours: leaving his luggage and guitar at a hotel in New York City, canceling a performance at Radio City, selling the ring he'd meant to use to propose. He was missing a performance where his dad would finally hear him sing. He didn't have his suit or any clothing other than what he wore, and now it looked as if the flight might not even leave before nightfall.

He calculated the losses as an accountant would write numbers in the debit column. Then he moved his mind to where he was going—not what he was leaving. He calmed himself thinking that he was going toward all that mattered, and he let go of everything else.

CHAPTER THIRTEEN

Christmas Day

> 'Tis afterwards that everything is understood.
>
> —OLD IRISH PROVERB

Charlotte awoke at midnight, the stars so close they seemed to fall from the sky and into her hotel room. She glanced at Kara sleeping in the next bed and thought of the line between married and single, between love and hate, between forgiveness and forgetting. Sometimes there isn't a line; there is just the lifting of fog or the accumulation of time and knowing. But in getting married there is a moment, a definite *before* and firm *after*.

185

She searched her mind for a time before she loved Jimmy and after she loved Jimmy, but there was no line, and if there was she didn't know she'd crossed it until it was behind her. Part of her wanted to go back to when she didn't love him. But then again, love changed her and there was that.

She closed her eyes and wondered how his concert was going in New York. He'd be singing right now, or about to get onstage. She sent him the love that filled her heart and closed her eyes.

The plane from JFK took off for Shannon ten hours late. Passengers were irritable and hungry; children were whining and old women grumbling. The flight attendants handed out free drinks and consoled the passengers that it was better to be safe than on time.

Jimmy settled back into his window seat at the very rear of the plane, directly against the back wall of the toilets. "Lucky me," he mumbled, and then remembered that, yes, he was lucky. This was the last seat.

The plane full and in flight, Jimmy settled back to try to sleep in a perfectly upright position with an older woman next to him, reading with her light on. He finally gave up and looked through the in-flight magazine to see what the movie would be.

"Aye," the woman next to him mumbled.

"Excuse me?" Jimmy asked.

She looked at him, and for the first time he noticed that her eyes were of the most brilliant green he'd ever seen. This made him smile.

"Did I speak out loud?" she asked in an Irish accent.

"Yes."

"The movie. I've seen it. I was hoping for something new. This flight is so long, and after all that waiting in the airport, now I'll barely make it home to spend any of Christmas with my husband."

"Do you live in Ireland?" Jimmy asked, thankful now for the distraction of someone else's life.

"I do. I was here visiting my son and grandchildren. But that's what I get for trying to be two places at once for Christmas."

"I know what you mean."

"Why are you visiting our fair isle?"

"My brother, he's getting married tomorrow." Jimmy stared out the window. "For him I guess it's today, because it's morning there. It's Christmas morning. His wedding morning."

"Ah," she said. "And here we are suspended in the sky."

"Exactly."

"Is your entire family already there?"

There was something in her eyes, in the lilt and fetch of her speech and smile that caused Jimmy to tell this old woman his *entire* story—to tell her about the song, the ring, the tour, the concert, his father, all of it, until the moment where he sat on that plane trying to get to his brother's wedding, to the woman he loved. That's how the long plane flight passed—in stories told and stories heard.

The morning arrived crisp and cold, the sky clear and the swans appearing to be dressed for the wedding, although Charlotte knew they dressed that way every morning. They were all ready, Kara's hair pulled up with loose curls falling down her back, her mother's veil in her hand.

The women gathered in Kara and Charlotte's room, sipping champagne and laughing, wishing one another Merry Christmas, and taking turns using the mirror to get ready.

Kara tilted her head back to let Rosie attach the veil. "If as a child I ever imagined my wedding day, I don't think I imagined us all cramped into a teeny hotel room sharing a single mirror and drinking champagne on Christmas Day."

Rosie hugged Kara from behind. "Isn't it great how even our own imaginations cannot conjure up the most perfect thing? It's so wonderful when it's better than we thought or imagined on our own."

Charlotte slipped the green silk dress over her slip and turned to her mother. "Can you zip me?"

Rosie spoke up. "Okay, I don't want to be all bossy, but we need to walk over to the church. It's time."

Bundled in scarves and coats, the women were a beautiful bouquet of wildflowers tumbling out of the hotel, walking the two blocks to the church. The morning was clear, the sky swept of stars and clouds, of anything at all but the single sun hanging on the far horizon. The bay shivered beneath the cold, no sweater or coat to warm it, exposed to the sky without protection. The swans flapped and danced, teasing one another and the shoreline. The Christmas lights strung from trees and light posts winked at the women as if they knew where they were going and what they were doing.

They burst through the back door of the church, now whispering and laughing in quiet tones as if the church had demanded this by its mere granite presence.

Iona was waiting and took their coats. "The first Christmas mass has taken place. There is one going on now and then the wedding. Are you ready?"

Kara nodded. "Yes."

"You are a beautiful bride," Iona said. "Radiant."

"Thanks. Are the guys here yet?"

"Yes, they're waiting in the back room, telling jokes I do not want to hear." She smiled. "All is well, I promise. I'll be back in about thirty minutes to take you into the sacristy."

Charlotte stepped forward. "Do you mind," she asked both Iona and Kara, "if I walk around to the entryway for a couple minutes?"

"Of course not," Kara said. "Why?"

Charlotte shrugged. She wanted to see Our Lady of Galway one more time. She wanted to touch the hem of her wooden skirt and see her face placid and still, her face that seemed to say all would be well. Yes, all would be well.

*J*immy stood at the rental car window ringing the bell for an employee. When the plane had landed he'd attempted to turn on his cell phone, only to find he had no service in Ireland—which was probably a good thing, as then he couldn't listen to the ten voice mails Milton had left for him. Finally, a young girl with purple hair and a nose ring came from behind the wall.

"Merry Christmas," Jimmy said, glancing at his watch

while digging into his pocket. "I need a car and map to Claddagh Village."

The girl ambled toward the computer. "I don't think we have any cars left. It's Christmas."

Jimmy groaned. The wedding would begin in an hour and a half, and the drive was almost exactly that. "Anything. I'll drive anything," he said.

She squinted at the screen. "There's nothing. And although you'd be saying you'd drive anything, there's nothing."

"There must be. Just one car. Just one."

She laughed. "Only my clunker, and you won't be wanting to drive that." Her sweet Irish accent made the word "clunker" sound like a good thing.

Jimmy leaned forward on the desk. "Okay, here's the deal. My brother's wedding starts in an hour and a half. I've gone through hell to get here. I left my luggage in New York, sat next to the airplane bathroom in a straight-up position for seven hours, and now I just need a car. That's all that's left. A car is all that's left between me and my brother's wedding."

Her eyes opened wide. "Really? Is all that true?"

He laughed. "Unfortunately, yes." He held out his cash. "I can give this to you, along with a promise of utmost sincerity that I will bring the car back as soon as the wedding is over."

"Hey," she said, "why don't I drive you? You can pay me to drive you, and then you won't have to return the car. I was on night shift, and I'm off now. I need an excuse to not see my family. My da is home for the holidays, and I'd like to be late for the day. What do you say?"

"Let's go." Jimmy smiled.

The purple-haired girl—her name was Lydia—drove them through the crisp Christmas morning.

"So, can you be telling me why your brother is getting married in Ireland and, of all places, the little fishing village of Claddagh?"

"It's kind of a complicated story, but it all had to do with this old lady who told his fiancée a story."

"What kind of story?"

"About the Claddagh ring and about her life. Jack's fiancée found Jack because of the story . . . "

The girl smiled and tapped her steering wheel. "Tell me."

Jack laughed. "You people and stories."

"That's our thing," she said.

"Well, this old lady, Maeve Mahoney, was in a nursing home and . . . "

The girl slammed on her brakes, pulled to the side of the road.

"What's wrong?" Jimmy pointed to the road.

"Say the name again."

He did.

She laughed this beautiful, melodic laugh that was more of a song than it was anything else. "That is my great-gram."

Jimmy shook his head. "This is just getting weirder and weirder."

She drove the car back onto the road. "Okay, I'll get you there, but you have to finish the story."

And so he did.

Lydia drove down the Claddagh Quay and then pointed. "That's the church."

Jimmy stared at the red granite structure in the morning sun, the beauty of it mirrored in the bay as if there were two churches, one of permanence and one of a dream world. He glanced at his watch and then at Lydia. "The wedding already started."

She stopped the car. "Well, then you'd better hurry."

Jimmy took that moment to look into her eyes. "I don't know how to thank you, but I will. I will."

"Ah, Great-Grand-Mam would tell me it was my privilege."

Jimmy threw open the car door and bolted for the front door. He entered with the wind behind his back, the cold forcing its way into the foyer. His sneakers squeaked on the marble, and he found himself face-to-face with Our Lady of Galway. He stared at her for the briefest moment, as if he knew her or had met her before, and then he looked toward the front of the church.

There they stood—Kara and Jack facing each other, Charlotte standing to the side, and Mr. Larson where he, Jimmy, should be. He took the longest breath and walked toward the aisle. He moved slowly, not knowing whether to speak or just slip into the pew.

It was Charlotte who first saw him, and she took in a sharp breath, her eyes opening wider, as if they needed to believe what they saw. Kara and Jack spun around, and the priest stopped in midsentence. Jack gave a timid wave and stopped midaisle, as if waiting for someone to tell him what to do. Sit? Run? Leave?

Kara nodded at Jack, as if to say, "Go to him."

Jack and Jimmy met halfway, where Jimmy spoke first. "I'm sorry. I am so, so sorry."

Jack hugged his brother, and then stepped back. "Merry Christmas."

Jimmy then hugged Kara before he turned to Charlotte with the hope of any man who turns to the woman he loves.

She smiled at him, bit her bottom lip in the way she does when she attempts to stop her tears. He held out his hand, and she took it, drawing him toward her. There were no words said because at that moment none were needed. The words—they would come later. Jimmy stepped back and took his place as best man.

Ah, the tears and joy mixed into that church were a sacred sacrament.

The front foyer of the church was crowded with the small gathering of Mr. and Mrs. Jack Sullivan and their friends and family. Kara's veil had been lifted from her face, and she held her husband's hand. Jimmy Sullivan stood in front of his brother and his friends and family and apologized once again.

"You're here—that is all that matters. You are here. No more apologies," Jack said.

"Look at me. I'm a mess. I probably ruined your nice wedding photographs." He motioned toward the photographer, who was snapping pictures of Charlotte, Deidre, and Rosie.

"I don't believe you've messed up anything, big brother. Except maybe . . . " Jack motioned toward Charlotte.

Jimmy nodded and then called Charlotte's name. She walked toward him, and together they stood in front of Kara and Jack, in front of Our Lady. A certain kind of hush fell over the foyer, the kind of hush that is full of expectation.

"Charlotte Lynn Carrington, I have never loved as I have loved you. I'm sorry I wasn't here. I'm sorry I lost sight of all I know, of you and our love." Jimmy dropped to one knee. "Will you be my wife?"

Charlotte dropped down to face him, kneeling next to him. "Yes," she whispered.

"I had a ring," he said, taking her hand, "but I sold it to get on the flight. At this moment, all I have to give you is my heart and a promise."

"That," Charlotte said, "is all I ever wanted." She placed her head on his shoulder, and he pulled her close, wrapped his arms around her, and held her as close as a man kneeling on a marble floor can hold a woman in a bridesmaid dress.

The small crowd clapped and whooped and made noises that at any other time would not seem appropriate in the church, but at that moment absolutely were. Then an older woman entered and glanced around the space until her green eyes lit like a lantern had been fired behind her pupils. "Mr. Sullivan?"

They all stopped and looked at her.

"Wow," Jimmy said. "Mrs. O'Brien. How did you get here?" It was the woman he had sat next to on the plane, the sweet woman who had listened to his story.

"I never did tell you that I am the Mrs. O'Brien of the Claddagh jeweler. The original Claddagh ring maker here in Galway."

Jimmy laughed. "I guess I shouldn't be surprised."

"And where is this Charlotte?"

Charlotte stepped forward. "I'm here."

The woman held her hand out to Jimmy and slipped something into his palm. "Now, do it right this time, son. This is a symbol of faith. Give it in that spirit." And she turned on her black shoes and pushed open the front door. By the time Jimmy looked into his hand and saw the Claddagh ring with the large emerald in the middle, Mrs. O'Brien was gone, as if she'd never been there. He turned to Charlotte, overwhelmed with the realization that sometimes hope is not only fulfilled, but filled to overflowing. He knew better now than any other not to turn away a gift. He slipped the ring on Charlotte's finger.

Together they stood, and when the hugging and tears were over, Jack shook his head and asked Jimmy, "How did you get here? What happened?"

"It was crazy, really." Jimmy looked around the foyer.

"First Dad showed up." He looked at Jack. "More on that later. And then there was a homeless angel and a child named Maria dressed like a guiding star and then a guy named Joe who got me on the flight. And then Maeve's great-granddaughter drove me to the church." He shook his head. "I'm still not sure how I got here."

Tears gathered in the corners of Kara's eyes like raindrops at the edge of a windowsill. "You'd think Maeve Mahoney had something to do with this, wouldn't you?"

Ahya, now I did, didn't I?

EMERALD ISLE SHORTBREAD

$3/4$ cup unsalted butter, softened

$1/4$ cup powdered sugar

$1/4$ cup granulated sugar

2 cups all-purpose flour

2 tbsp. green decorative sugar for sprinkling

Preheat oven to 375 degrees. Line an 8 x 8-inch baking pan with parchment paper or a Silpat mat. Beat the butter in a mixer or food processor for about 2 minutes, or until it is light in color. Gradually beat in the sugar until the mixture is soft in texture. Stir in the flour to make a softened dough. It will be crumbly.

Pack the dough, $3/4$ to 1 inch thick, in the lined pan. Cover with plastic wrap, and then use the back of a teaspoon to level the dough and smooth the top as necessary. Remove plastic wrap.

Mark off $1\frac{1}{2}$-inch squares in the dough, and cut down between each square to make it easier to remove after they are baked. Bake for 15–20 minutes in the middle of the oven until light golden brown, opening oven a few minutes before finished and removing pan quickly to sprinkle shortbread with green sugar.

Move to a rack to cool before removing the pre-cut bars. Store for 2–3 weeks in an airtight container or freeze.

Recipe by Nathalie Dupree, TV Host and Cookbook Writer

CHARLOTTE'S SOUTHERN GARLAND

Materials:

    Evergreen trimmings

    Twine

    #24 Floral Wire

    Your favorite added decorations (ex: dried pomegranates,
       mercury ornaments, magnolia leaves, etc. . . .)

1. Gather your favorite evergreen trimmings. The more you gather, the longer and fuller the garland will be. (Charlotte spent hours wandering the back woods of her mama's house, piling her wheelbarrow high and wide with juniper, pine and magnolia.)

2. Now gather the things you want to add to the evergreen. (Charlotte used dried pomegranates and mercury Christmas ornaments.) Choose whatever strikes your fancy and will be a compliment to your holiday design! Set these decorations aside with your magnolia leaves.

3. Pile all your beautiful trimmings and then begin to cut your trimmings into approximately six-inch pieces.

4. Now cut a ten-foot length of your twine. Lay this twine straight on a flat surface and then tie a loop into one end of it.

5. Pick up your #24 floral wire and attach it to the loop. DON'T cut your wire yet—keep it on the spool so you can unwind the wire as you go along.

6. Gather a handful of evergreen trimmings and loop the floral wire around the ends of this bundle. Now face the bunch with

continues

the stems facing from the twine-loop and then attach the ever-green to the twine by wrapping the floral wire around the end of the bundles. Continue looping the wire around the bundles of evergreen, bunching bundles as close together as possible. (Don't forget—the stems face the end with the loop where you started.)

7. Continue attaching the evergreen bundles all the way down the twine until you reach the end, filling in the length and sides until it is as full as you'd like it.

8. Now cut the wire.

9. Use the floral wire to attach the dried pomegranates, magnolia leaves, or mercury ornaments to your taste.

10. Hang and then smile at your beautiful handmade garland.

A CONVERSATION WITH
PATTI CALLAHAN HENRY

What inspired this story?

I was fascinated with the idea that someone would finally reach a "perfect" goal—the thing they thought would be The Answer to happiness, only to discover that the "perfect" thing made life more difficult as they lost sight of what matters most.

The main characters in this novel—Jimmy Sullivan and Charlotte Carrington—are the brother and best friend of the main characters in my novel *When Light Breaks*. Through the years, I've received letters from readers asking me "What happened to Jimmy and Charlotte? Did Kara and Jack get married?" So this book is dedicated, in many ways, to those readers. Because they asked what happened to these characters, I felt the need to answer.

So this book was inspired by two questions—what happened to the characters from *When Light Breaks*, and what happens when someone gets everything they believed they wanted? Further inspiration comes from my deep fascination with myth, legend, and the ability of a story to change a life for the better.

A song is at the core of this story. Are you a songwriter? Why did you choose to have a song change Jimmy's life?

No, I'm not a songwriter, but I wish I were. I do. I really do. I've tried. I'm fascinated with the best songwriters—the ones who can reveal in one refrain what takes me an entire novel to say. I believe that any "story"—whether told in song, myth, legend, novel, fairytale, or poem—can change a life.

I believe story is a search for truth, a language of mystery that somehow reveals meaning. Therefore Jimmy's song—which is really a story—does offer the truth, does change his life.

Both Charlotte and Kara have "creative" jobs. Can you comment on this choice?

There are certain things that can bind friends together—history, trauma, location—but what brought and bound Kara and Charlotte together were their creative spirits. I believe that we all are creative, yet sometimes people make the choice to stifle their creativity in the name of acceptance or success. Any job—any job whatsoever—is creative if we allow our spirits to make it so. Yet, mostly we are worried about what other people think or what our families think. If we stifle our creativity, I believe we can become depressed, feel stuck.

Being "creative" in a venue we love—writing, painting, poetry, etc.—can be very scary, because if we are truly expressing our creativity, then we are truly expressing our inner selves, and for most of us this is a scary thing to do! So for those who choose to leave a traditional job behind to pursue a creative passion, there is a lot of fear. I believe that the arts—writing, painting, poetry, photography—tell us the truth about our lives much more so than the "facts" of our lives.

Part of this story—*The Perfect Love Song*—is about just this: how an artistic expression of truth can change a life. How a story doesn't have to be "factual" to be true. And this miracle is part of a creative life.

Who was your favorite character to write in *The Perfect Love Song*? Why?

My favorite character—ayha—that's like asking which of my children I love the most. But IF I must choose, then I will have to say that the narrator's voice is my favorite "character" because she wrote this novella in her usual witty, wise voice. I love how she was able to step back as a watcher and tell the story as an outsider, yet as someone who loved the characters with fierce loyalty.

How much of a person's character would you say is shaped by his or her childhood?

In the novel I am writing now, I say this "Words have a way—I know now—of working their way into a soul and forming that soul into a shape and vessel it might not have otherwise been. How many times can a mother tell a daughter what is and is not good for her and that daughter not believe it?"

So, yes, I believe that in many ways our childhoods shape who and what we become. This shaping comes through where we live, the words spoken into our souls, the atmosphere we are surrounded by (love or fear), etc. . . .

When I am asked WHY I became a writer, I often say, "That's a love story." And what I mean is that I came to writing *through* the things I loved as a child—books, libraries, words, and story. If I'd had a different childhood, or different parents, or had never moved in adolescence, would I be the same person or the same writer I am now? Probably not.

When the group of friends arrive in Ireland, they are awed by the majesty of Galway bay. Have you been to Ireland and did you base any of your settings on actual places there?

Yes, I have been to Ireland three times (the number of magic). The first time I visited, I was in college and I went with my parents and sisters. The next two times I went with my husband and daughter, Meagan, who was an Irish dancer.

The places I describe are real; the characters' overwhelming feelings of awe and grandeur were my impressions exactly. I saw and felt the greenest green, the formidable bay, the overpowering cliffs and the sense of ancient power that permeates this country, and I only hope the reader can sense and taste this mystery.

I have not been to the church in Galway—Church of St. Mary on the Hill—but I describe it in detail through the photos and historical accounts of this fascinating Dominican church. The St. Mary statue in the sacristy is also authentic and her story is full of mystery and myth combined. I can only hope that I wrote of both the church and the statue with enough truth to guard the integrity of their stories.

You create characters like Jimmy, who, though flawed, also evoke sympathy. Throughout your life, have you met people who are this way? What draws you to write about characters like this?

I don't ever intentionally base any of my characters on people I know. But I do offer this caveat: I only know what I know. Not one of my characters is based on someone I know (so far) or on myself. Although these stories might not be about me, they are from me, from somewhere inside me.

My characters are "created" as individuals, as someone separate from a preconceived notion of a living (or deceased) person, yet I'm quite sure that mannerisms, quirks, experiences, and traits of people I love work their way into my characters' lives and personalities. I just don't do it on purpose . . .

I don't know exactly why I'm drawn to the hurting and wounded character other than my need to write my way into their healing and redemption. I approach a story from only one angle: "I wonder what's going to happen next," because therein lies hope. In knowing that something—anything—can happen next, the character then has a chance for healing, or for love, for or something new.

I believe hopelessness (a desperate condition of the heart) comes from thinking that "things will never change." So I write my characters, and then I take them to places where they are given a chance to make a new choice, to do something different and maybe love again. I am annoyingly hopeful, and yet I know there are conditions and situations of the soul that are sad and desperate. I desire the way of healing, and story is my meager attempt to create this pathway with words.

An intergenerational friendship is key to your story. How have you been significantly influenced by someone quite a few years older than yourself?

I think sometimes I write about things I WISH had happened to me. I don't believe I do this on purpose, but I often create women who live in small towns, have never moved, and live in a close-knit small town community, which of course never happened to me. I moved around when I was young and I've always lived in large cities (Philadelphia, Fort Lauderdale, and Atlanta). So, although there have been many, many people who have influenced my life, I haven't had that one "mentor" who is older and wiser and has guided my life. Although I wish for one!

In this novel, the absent father makes himself felt in the holes he has created in his sons' lives. Why did you choose to have Jimmy and Jack come from a broken home?

I didn't choose to have them come from a broken home; they arrived on the page that way. Okay, I know I wrote it, but they came to me from a broken home. They were wounded and trying to find their way in the world the best they could.

I often find myself writing about injured souls and how they find a way to heal and move through the world in a creative and healing way. Love, I believe, is often the catalyst for a new life and I explore the myriad ways this occurs—love of music, of story, of life, of a person—love at all really.

DISCUSSION GUIDE

1. What do you think of the title *The Perfect Love Song*? Do you think such a song can exist? Why do you think the author only gives us the first few lines of the song? Try your hand at writing one and see what you think of the results!

2. In this story, the song that was so "perfect" had a negative effect on Jimmy's life. Have you ever had something "perfect" come into your life, only to understand the negative influence it has on you or your loved ones?

3. Chapter one begins with the traditional Irish storyteller's opening, "May stillness be upon your thoughts and silence upon your tongue! For I tell you a tale that was told at the beginning . . . the one story worth telling . . . " The Irish have a rich cultural history of storytelling and of myths passed down from generation to generation much the way Maeve tells Kara her love story. Are all stories interconnected in some way? Do you think many modern stories are actually based on far more ancient tales and myths? And if so, what are some examples?

4. Callahan Henry's fiction is a celebration of Southern low country culture and customs. You can often feel a novel's setting through

the actual words used in telling the tale, the beauty in the language as it captures the spirit or energy of the characters, or the smell of the sea and salty air. What is unique about the setting of this book, and how did it enhance the story? How much do you feel that the narrative voice is both affected and informed by place? And how does the use of sea imagery like the small shell Charlotte brings with her to the church in Ireland play into the narrative?

5. At one point in the novel, the narrator says "There are so many things that work themselves into chance." How do chance and destiny affect the characters in the novel as they make decisions and live and love? Do you agree that real life is the result of pre-determined forces? Or can we affect our fate?

6. The author writes about complex characters finding their place in the world, of the love and heartache in friendship, and of family and home. How do characters change or evolve throughout the course of the story? What events trigger such changes? Where do you see these characters in six months?

7. Jimmy and Jack had very difficult childhoods, and we learn that they were in fact abused by their alcoholic father. How does the past imprint their present-day lives and hinder their futures? Are they ever able to escape the effects of the past, and, if so, by what means?

8. When Jimmy tells Jack he will miss the wedding ceremony, Jack remarks "That's just great. Jimmy, always in time for the party." How does the concept of responsibility toward family play into the novel? Weddings are often a time of joy but also of incredible stress for families. What do you think it is about weddings in

particular that can bring families closer together, or tear them apart?

9. The Claddagh ring appears throughout the novel. What is it about the ring that symbolizes the themes of love returning, reconciliation, and rebirth? How does this play into Jimmy's conversation with his father? How does Jimmy's need for his father's approval and his reunion with his father influence Jimmy to return to Charlotte's side?

10. The story outcome is greatly influenced by Maeve Mahoney, her stories, and her advice. Do you believe that those who have passed on influence our lives and choices? If so, how?

11. Music is an important theme throughout the novel. Music becomes a father to Jimmy and Jack when their father is not in their lives, and in turn, their band also becomes their family. How does involving yourself in art or music help to fill the void of a close personal relationship that is now lost? Do you think that music and art can be viable replacements for lost love? Or are music and art outlets for grief and loss?

12. The holiday season features prominently in *The Perfect Love Song*, and it is Christmas that brings everyone back together in the end. At one point, when Kara and Charlotte visit the nursing home, the narrator says, "Giving means having more." How do you give back during the holiday season? Are there ways that we can inspire others to remember to visit the elderly in our communities and to truly understand that giving is a gift in and of itself?

Enjoy a reading sample from *New York Times* bestselling author Kat Martin's most romantic and inspirational story

The Christmas Clock

A NOVEL BY
KAT MARTIN

Published by Vanguard Press
Available in mass market paperback
October 2010 for a special gift price of
$5.99 U.S. / $7.99 CAN
wherever books are sold

Prologue

◇◇◇◇◇◇◇◇◇◇◇◇◇◇◇◇

There are years in our lives that change us, mold us forever in some way. I was eight years old that Christmas, too young to really understand all the undercurrents swirling around me.

It is only now, fourteen years later, as I graduate from Michigan State University and prepare for a job in the health care industry, that I am able to look back with the clarity to see that Christmas for the miracle it truly was.

Back then, during that summer of 1994, with the trees leafed out and the sun warming my shoulders through a T-shirt that hung down to my knees, I didn't realize disaster lay just a few months ahead. I only knew I wanted to buy the beautiful clock in the window of Tremont's Antiques as a gift for my grandmother, Lottie Sparks.

I didn't know that in trying to buy the clock, I would meet the people who would change my world, and my life would never be the same.

CHAPTER ONE

August 1994

〈◇◇◇◇◇◇◇◇◇◇◇◇◇◇◇◇◇◇◇〉

*S*ylvia Winters was going home. She had only been back to the small Michigan town of Dreyerville once in the past eight years. Her mother's funeral had demanded a return, but she had left the following day. Only a few close friends had attended the brief, graveside service held at the Greenhaven Cemetery. Marsha Winters had started drinking the day her husband disappeared. Abandoned with a month-old baby in a ramshackle house at the edge of town, she took up the bottle and didn't put it down for twenty years. Neither she nor Syl ever saw Syl's father again.

Times had been hard back then, but the years Syl had spent in the charming rural community surrounded by forested, rolling hills held memories she cherished. She was a good student, and she was popular. In high school, a glowing future spread out before her: a scholarship to college and a career in nursing, a husband and children, the sort of life Syl had always dreamed of and never had.

But life was never predictable, she had learned, and oftentimes cruel. At nineteen, during her first year at Dreyerville Community College, Syl had fallen in love. She and Joe Dixon, the school's star quarterback, were engaged to be married the summer of the following year. Syl couldn't imagine ever being happier.

Then her world came crashing down around her, and all of her dreams along with it. A routine doctor's appointment had brought news so grim that the week before the ceremony, Syl called off the wedding. She packed her belongings that same afternoon and left for Chicago.

If it hadn't been for her mother's sister, Bessie, Syl wasn't sure she would have made it. Aunt Bess and Syl's dearest friend, Mary McGinnis Webster, had been responsible for getting her through the most difficult time of her life.

But things were different now.

Syl studied the double yellow line in the middle of the two-lane highway leading into Dreyerville. The air conditioner hummed inside the car, while outside, the temperature was hot and a little humid this late in the summer. Dense growths of leafy green trees lined both sides of the road, and a narrow stream wove its way through the grasses, bubbling and frothing in places, lazy and meandering in others.

As she drove her newly washed white Honda Civic toward the turn onto Main Street, a feeling of homecoming expanded in her chest. She recognized Barnett's Feed and Seed, just down the road from Murdock's Auto Repair at the edge of town.

Making a left onto Main, she spotted the old domed courthouse built in 1910 and the ornate clock tower in the middle of the grassy town square. A little farther down the street, Culver's Dry Cleaning held the middle spot in the long, two-story brick building that filled the block on the left, and there was Tremont's Antiques, right next to Brenner's Bakery.

Sylvia smiled. The apartment she had just rented sat above the garage at Doris Culver's house. Doris worked at Brenner's Bakery, had for years. The middle-aged woman was practically a fixture behind the counter of the shop.

Syl's friend Mary had found her the apartment. A job as a nurse in a local doctor's office had recently appeared in the employment section of the Dreyerville *Morning News*, and Mary had convinced her to send in an application. After flying out for an interview, Sylvia had gotten the job.

She was coming home at last. She wasn't sure what sort of life she could make for herself in the town she once had fled, but something told her coming back was the only way she could conquer the demons that had haunted her for the past eight years.

• • •

Doris Culver didn't believe in happily ever after. She hadn't since she was nineteen, madly in love, and found her boyfriend, Ronnie Munns, in the backseat of his parent's '55 Chevy with Martha Gladstone, the local librarian. Love, Doris believed after that, was for fools and dreamers, and she never allowed herself to succumb to its lure again.

At fifty-six, Doris Culver felt old, but then she had for most of her life. Her husband, Floyd, the retired owner of Culver's Dry Cleaning, was a nondescript, balding man who wore horn-rimmed glasses and built birdhouses to fill up his empty days. Floyd was six years older than Doris, whom he had met when she came into his store with an armload of laundry. After cleaning her clothes for nearly five years, Floyd asked Doris out on a date. This July fifth, they had celebrated twenty-two years of marriage.

Doris felt as if it were fifty.

She rarely saw her husband except at dinner, which he ate mostly in silence. Afterward, he returned to his wood-shop in the garage at the back of the house, where he stayed until he trudged up to bed at exactly nine P.M.

Though the sale of Floyd's business three years ago had provided them with a comfortable living, Doris had kept her job at the bakery, where she had been employed for years. She loved her job, especially decorating the cakes and cookies the shop made for holidays and other special occasions. With little else to fill her time, she went to work early and usually stayed past closing. Afterward, she returned to her two-bedroom, white stucco house on Maple Street, cooked Floyd's dinner, cleared the dishes, and spent the rest of the evening painting ceramics.

It was a consuming hobby. Every table, every book-shelf, even the window sills, held miniature clowns, birds, horses, dogs, cats, vases, and pitchers all done in the bright colors Doris used in an effort to cheer up her lonely world. Instead, somehow the crowded rows of objects, often in need of dusting, only made the house more oppressive.

Doris was glad for the hours she spent at the bakery, where the fragrant aroma of chocolate-chip cookies and fresh-baked bread was enough to buoy her spirits. The shop on Main next to Tremont's Antiques was a narrow brick building with big picture windows painted with the name Brenner's Bakery in wide, sculpted gold letters. Frank Brenner had died sixteen years ago, but the bakery, now owned by his son, remained a landmark in Dreyerville.

It was Saturday morning. Doris stood behind the counter wiping crumbs off the top when the bell chimed above the door, indicating the arrival of a customer. She tucked a strand of gray hair dyed blond under her pink and white cap and smiled at her next-door neighbor and her grandson, Lottie and Teddy Sparks, as they walked into the shop.

"Good morning," Doris beamed. "How are you and Teddy today?"

Lottie set her shopping bag down on a little iron chair. "Darned arthritis has been acting up some, but aside from that, both of us are fine." She looked down with affection at her grandson. "We're kind of hungry, though." Lottie was wrinkled and slightly stoop-shouldered and her hair was as white as paper. Still, there was always a sparkle in her eyes and the hint of rose in her cheeks.

Doris smiled. "Well, we can certainly take care of that." She turned toward the dark-haired, fair-skinned boy, who looked up at her with big brown, soulful eyes. "So what's it going to be, Teddy? A glazed or a maple bar?" It was a Saturday morning tradition. Doris always looked forward to seeing Lottie, who had once been her fifth-grade teacher.

The pair lived in the yellow and white wood-framed house on Maple Street next door to Doris, but they didn't get to visit much, not with the hours Doris worked. But she had always admired Lottie Sparks, and Teddy was purely a treasure.

The child stared into the case that was filled with donuts: jelly, chocolate frosted with walnuts, powdered, and crumb. There were also bear claws and all manner of coffee cake rings. He nibbled his lower lip, then pointed toward the top shelf of the case.

"A maple bar, please."

"My, that does sound good." Doris plucked a piece of waxed paper from the box on the counter, reached into the case, and drew out a fat, maple-frosted bar. "Here you go, Teddy."

The little boy grinned. "Thank you, Mrs. Culver."

Lottie ordered a cinnamon roll, and Doris handed it over on another sheet of waxed paper. When Lottie turned to leave, Doris reminded her that she had forgotten to pay for her purchase.

"Silly of me." Lottie reached into her handbag for the little plastic coin purse she always carried. She asked again how much she owed, then dug through the money to find the right change, fumbling with this coin and that until she finally put the money up on the counter and Doris picked out the sum she needed.

Doris watched the woman cross the room, feeling a hint of concern. Lottie was getting more and more forgetful. Doris couldn't help wondering what would happen to Teddy if the old woman's memory continued to get worse.

The pair sat down at one of the small, round tables in front of the window to savor their purchases, and Doris watched with only a small twinge of jealousy as the boy looked up and smiled so sweetly at his grandmother.

When Doris had married Floyd at thirty-four, she was already too old to have a child, or at least she had thought so at the time. Floyd, whose two boys by a previous marriage were living with their mother in Florida, didn't really care. Occasionally, Doris wondered if, all those years ago, she had made the right decision, but deep down she knew that she was never cut out to raise a child.

Grandmother and grandson finished their treats and got up from the little round table. Doris waved good-bye as they tossed their used waxed paper and napkins into the trash can and walked out the door. She thought of Teddy and the mother he had lost four years ago, the reason he now lived with Lottie. If he lost his grandmother as well . . .

She shook her head, worried what the boy's future might hold.

• • •

Lottie exchanged places with her grandson on the sidewalk, positioning herself between him and the light passage of Dreyerville traffic on Main Street. At seventy-one, Lottie never would have suspected she would be raising an eight-year-old boy, though it shouldn't have surprised her.

Her only daughter, Wilma, had never been the responsible sort. In her early teens, Wilma had run away from home more than once. She missed school, and started smoking in secret when she was fourteen. Lottie found her drunk the first time two years later. The girl had graduated high school by the sheer force of Lottie's will, though she never went on to college as Lottie had hoped.

Instead, at the age of thirty-seven, after two failed marriages and a string of deadbeat, live-in boyfriends, Wilma had wound up pregnant by the married man she was dating. Four years later, after drinking and partying with a friend, she had lost control of her car on her way home and died when she hit a tree.

Lottie had wound up with Teddy, but he wasn't a burden. The boy had become the joy of her life.

As they walked along the sidewalk, she felt his small hand in hers and smiled. Glancing ahead, her steps began to slow and Teddy came to a halt beside her. Both of them looked into the window of Tremont's Antiques, a favorite place to visit on their Saturday morning outings. Today, they didn't go in, but Lottie could see the small Victorian hand-painted clock she had been admiring for nearly a year.

"It's still there, Gramma."

"Yes, I see it is." Lottie loved clocks. She owned four beautiful antique clocks she had purchased over the years and a big grandfather clock her late husband, Chester, had bought for her on their fortieth wedding anniversary.

But this little clock was special. It reminded her of the one her mother had on the wall in the kitchen when she was a little girl. She used to sit at the old oak table and watch the hands move over the face while her mother baked cookies. The clock at Tremont's reminded her of the happy days of her childhood, memories that were rapidly fading.

Lottie's chest tightened with sudden despair. Something terrible was happening to her, something she couldn't fight and simply could not stop.

Two years ago, she had been diagnosed with Alzheimer's disease. At first the signs were subtle: misplacing objects, forgetting the date right after she had looked at the calendar, not remembering little words like *cat* or *comb*, saying another word in its place. Worried, she had gone to see her longtime family physician, Dr. Waller. He had referred her to a doctor named Davis, who specialized in Alzheimer's cases.

Several visits that included a medical history of her family, a physical examination, a brain scan, and a mental status evaluation revealed the truth. She had a very progressive form of Alzheimer's, a type of dementia that destroyed brain cells and robbed the mind of memory. She could expect the symptoms to worsen at a very rapid pace, and she needed to be prepared. Eventually, the disease would kill her.

Lottie looked down at Teddy, who was staring up at her with big, worried, brown eyes.

"Gramma? Are you all right?"

How long had she been standing there? She had no idea. She managed a smile for Teddy. "I'm fine, sweetheart. Why don't we go on home?"

Teddy looked relieved. Lottie gazed off down the street, which suddenly seemed less familiar. Their house was located two blocks farther down Main, then left on Maple Street. So far, she hadn't forgotten how to get there, but the doctors had warned her it could happen.

Teddy took her hand as they started walking. She let him lead the way. She wondered if he had noticed the subtle changes coming over her, and she suspected that he had. Lottie was a deeply religious woman. She was ready to meet her maker, though she would have preferred another path to glory. She would go without complaint, but there was Teddy to consider.

Her husband had passed away eight years ago. Her sister and daughter were dead. She had some distant cousins, but they were more feeble than she and certainly not suitable parents for an eight-year-old boy. For the past two years, ever since she had learned of her condition, Lottie had been hoping to find an answer to the problem of Teddy's future.

Before it was too late, she had to find Teddy a home.